THE ICE CHIPS AND THE HAUNTED HURRICANE

Roy MacGregor and Kerry MacGregor
Illustrations by Kim Smith

HarperTrophyCanada
An imprint of HarperCollinsPublishersLtd

Published by Harper*Trophy*Canada™,
an imprint of HarperCollins Publishers Ltd

First published by HarperCollins Publishers Ltd in a hardcover edition: 2018
This Harper*Trophy*Canada™ trade paperback edition: 2020

HarperCollins books may be purchased for educational, business,
or sales promotional use through our Special Markets Department.

HarperCollins Publishers Ltd
Bay Adelaide Centre, East Tower
22 Adelaide Street West, 41st Floor
Toronto, Ontario, Canada
M5H 4E3

www.harpercollins.ca

Library and Archives Canada Cataloguing in Publication
Title: The Ice Chips and the haunted hurricane / Roy MacGregor
and Kerry MacGregor.
Names: MacGregor, Roy, 1948- author. | MacGregor, Kerry, author. |
Smith, Kim, 1986- illustrator.
Description: Illustrated by Kim Smith. | Originally published: Toronto
Ontario, Canada : HarperCollins Publishers Ltd., ©2018.
Identifiers: Canadiana 20200173480 | ISBN 9781443452328 (softcover)
Classification: LCC PS8575.G84 I338 2020 | DDC jC813/.54—dc23

Printed and bound in the United States o America
LSC/H 9 8 7 6 5 4 3 2 1

For the coaches whose players sometimes wonder
where practice will get them.
—ROY MACGREGOR AND KERRY MACGREGOR

For all the time travellers out there.
—KIM SMITH

CHAPTER 1
Location Unknown

Blackness . . .

Thick as soup.

And it was rocking. The darkness was moving.

In front of Lucas Finnigan's eyes danced a greenish blur, as if he'd been staring at a bright white surface just before the lights went out—just before he'd been sucked into this . . .

Night? Is this night?

Lucas moved his head to shake away the darkness, to free his eyes. But the darkness didn't move. It clung to him like a damp facecloth.

Where am I?!

"Do you smell that?" Nica Bertrand's voice was shaky. Lucas's couldn't see her—the goalie he knew better as "Swift"—but he knew she was close. "Is it . . . dirt—*the smell*? Mud or something?"

Lucas slid his hand across the floor until he touched Swift's. Once she felt his hand, she gripped it tightly.

How could we have been so stupid to try this again?

"It's . . . *salt*," Ekamjeet Singh said slowly. Lucas's best friend and the teammate he called "Edge" was somewhere in front of Lucas and Swift, somewhere in the blackness. "The air smells like . . . the ocean."

The ocean?!

Lucas brought his hands to his moist cheeks. He closed his eyes tightly, and then opened them again. Slowly, they were starting to adjust to the darkness.

His sluggish brain was unscrambling, too . . .

Scratch had resurfaced the rink with his magical flood, just like last time, and the three Ice Chips had stepped out onto the ice.

We skated hard and fast. We hit the centre line . . .

And then, just like last time, Lucas, Edge, and Swift had leaped through time.

Now they were—well, they could be anywhere, really.

"We're . . . moving," Swift said.

Lucas looked up and saw the outline of a small round window. Through it, he could see a smudge of light, all on its own in the dark sky, like the only street lamp in a city gone black.

The moon!

"We're on a boat. Try Crunch!" Lucas whispered, remembering their plan. If they could reach Sebastián Strong—the defenceman they'd nicknamed "Crunch" because he was so nuts about numbers—they'd be okay. Crunch had stayed behind at the rink with his tablet, and with his help, they might be able to figure out where they were and what year they'd landed in.

Edge's comm-band walkie-talkie crackled to life, but when he said "12" into it—Crunch's number— no one answered. Either their comm-bands weren't working, or Crunch was just too far away.

"*Zilch-o-nada*," said Edge, using one of his made-up words to hide his disappointment. "No Crunch!"

"We're alone out here," said Swift, seeming even more tense than before. She began taking off her skates and searching the floor with her hands. She was trying to find her backpack. For this leap—their second one—all three Ice Chips had brought backpacks, and they'd all brought boots to change into. This time, they'd come prepared.

At least, they thought they had.

"We can't call home, but we can't be *completely* alone out here," Lucas said, trying to be encouraging.

He hurried into his second boot, slipping into his sock a jackknife he'd packed—just in case—before zipping up his bag. The wind coming through the cracks in the small room had gotten colder. It was as though the air, and everything in it, had become electric. Was there a storm coming?

"Of course we're not alone. Someone has to be steering the b—" Edge started. But suddenly the boat pitched sideways, throwing Lucas and his teammates with it.

It had lurched to the left, as if it had been taken by a wave and was about to keel over.

Edge, who'd been standing, slammed against a wall—or maybe a door—just as a handful of life jackets and fishing nets rained down onto Lucas's and Swift's heads. Lucas gripped Swift's hockey jersey with one hand and planted his other on the floor to keep from sliding sideways. The boat tried to right itself, but instead it pitched hard in the other direction.

"Ugh!" Swift called as she rolled backwards.

"Cover your heads!" Edge shouted.

A fishing pole detached from the wall and fell with a bang. A heavy utility box slid across the floor, just missing Swift's prosthetic leg.

BZZZZ-SHEEEP-ZZZZ!

It was Edge's comm-band!

"*Hello? Hello? Is somebody . . . there? Are you . . . in troub—? Hello?*" The voice was fuzzy, unsure. And words were dropping out of the signal. It wasn't Crunch—so who?

"It's *a kid*!" said Lucas, pushing a life jacket off his head and staring at Edge's comm.

He realized that a dim light was now flooding the box-like room they were in. The sun was coming up. The door that Edge had banged up against had swung open, and now they could see the mess of life jackets and fishing nets that had tumbled all around them.

"Wait! This boat isn't going to—?" Edge didn't want to finish his sentence. He didn't have to. The boat pitched to the left again, and the Ice Chips tried to grab on to whatever they could. A storm wasn't coming—*it was here*. And it was huge.

Through the open door, Lucas could see dark waves rising, threatening.

They were trying to pull the boat under!

Should we call for help? Blow whistles? Fire a flare gun?

Lucas pulled on a life jacket and scrambled for the buckle just as another huge wave hit. This time, the three Ice Chips went flying toward some storage shelves. Luckily, they were all still wearing their hockey helmets.

"*Hello? Hell—o?*" the young, static-filled voice called out over Edge's comm-band. Edge lifted his wrist up to his mouth, but then stared blankly at Lucas. What could he say that would help them?

"We've got to get to the steering wheel!" cried Swift, trying to be heard above the violent wind that was whipping against the side of the boat. Sharp raindrops were now flying in through the open door in sheets.

We've reached a kid, thought Lucas. *But who is he? And* where *is he?*

"*Be careful . . . There's a hurri . . . cane . . . coming! And it's—*" the voice continued over the comm-band.

"The kid—if he can hear us," Edge yelled, "he can get help!"

"See, we aren't alone!" Lucas called to Swift.

"OF COURSE YOU'RE NOT!" boomed a gruff voice, just as the light pouring into the storage room went out.

CHAPTER 2
Another Unknown Location: The Others

"Mom, this walkie-talkie's not working. Where's the other one?" a boy yelled as he sped down the stairs into the dimly lit basement. He was moving fast, but he didn't fall. He knew this path far too well and leaped athletically down the last few steps.

"Mom, where do I look?"

As the boy's mother yelled back that it was down there somewhere, Bond's heart began to beat so loudly that she could barely think. She'd never been so scared, so completely disoriented.

What in the world just happened? How did we get—?

As the kid hurried across the basement, Bond and Mouth Guard scrambled to tuck themselves into a dark corner of the room.

We have to stay hidden until we figure this out, Bond thought as she looked, wide-eyed, at Mouth

Guard and tried to slow her breathing. She didn't want her fear to give them away.

Mouth Guard opened his mouth, as though about to ask a question, but she glared back at him, warning that for once in his life, he'd better keep his lips zipped.

Her mind was racing. A minute ago, she and Mouth Guard had watched three Ice Chips step onto the ice at the community arena. And then . . . *what*?

Crunch, the team's technology whiz, had been in the stands, filming with his tablet. Lucas, Edge, and Swift had been on the ice. The three of them had pushed off skating, wearing backpacks and holding hands, just as Bond and Mouth Guard—two of the team's newest members—opened the door in the boards.

Bond's and Mouth Guard's blades touched the ice only an instant before the other skaters reached the centre line and . . .

No, it was too wild—too impossible.

They vanished?

Bond remembered hearing Crunch yell something. She remembered the feel of her skates scratching a perfect ice surface as she chased after her friends. But then?

Her brain was scrambled. Mouth Guard, who was now slowly, quietly pulling over a well-used hockey

net with a blue tarp taped to the back, looked confused, too.

He must be trying to shield us from the kid's view,
Bond thought, relieved that one Ice Chip was still with
her—even if they had no idea where they were.

The objects around them in the basement were
old—the hockey logos on the posters, the styles of
shoes, and the toys—but at the same time, everything
looked new. It didn't make any sense.

Bond quickly scanned her memory again. She and
Mouth Guard, both dressed in full gear, had arrived
at the rink for the same reason—to skate. But Bond
had also had something big—and difficult—to tell her
teammates. Something that meant everything. She'd
been thinking about it and, well, crying about it for
days.

Then, when Swift, Edge, and Lucas crossed that
centre line and vanished, Bond, who was always looking after other people, including her three younger sis-
ters, had acted on instinct.

She'd gone after them.

*That had definitely happened. We were on the ice.
My skate blades are still cold.*

There'd been a flash of light.

THE ICE CHIPS AND THE HAUNTED HURRICANE

A swirling motion, like they were being pulled down a drain.

The light had gotten brighter and brighter, and then Bond and Mouth Guard had landed here—wherever they were—on a pile of old hockey equipment on some kid's concrete basement floor.

Kah-SHHHHHHHHHHHH!

The walkie-talkie went off again.

"Are you still . . . *there? Hey*—hello? Hello?" The kid fumbled with the small plastic device in his hand, but there was nothing but static coming from the other end. Desperate, he continued going through storage boxes, opening cupboards, and checking the pockets of old coats, looking for the other walkie-talkie.

As quietly as she could, Bond grabbed Mouth Guard by his shoulder pads and pulled him toward her, tighter into the dark corner made by the hockey net and the basement wall.

"Where *are* we?" she mouthed. But inside her head, she was screaming: *Where are Swift, Edge, and Lucas? Why aren't we with them?*

Since Bond and Mouth Guard were new to the team, they didn't have comm-bands. They had no way of reaching anyone.

Tianna Foster—or "Bond," as the Chips had started calling her after hockey tryouts a few weeks ago—was used to moving around. She'd gone from Jamaica, where she was born and where she'd got her "James Bond" nickname playing roller derby, to Chicago, and then to Riverton. She knew very well how to deal with being dropped into a new place. But moving through a black hole? She had no way to judge how much danger they were in.

Neither did Dylan Chung.

Dylan, who always said whatever came into his head, had become "Mouth Guard" at tryouts after Bond had joked that he should wear a mouth guard full time—to keep the words from spilling out of his mouth. Now, hiding silently in the shadows beside a washer and dryer, he just looked frightened.

"I can't hear you anymore! Is it the *hurricane*?" the kid suddenly shouted, holding the walkie-talkie up to his mouth again. He was surprised when it had gone off in his room a few moments ago, but shocked when he'd learned that the person on the other end was actually in trouble.

Bond and Mouth Guard stayed frozen, listening to the static. The boy flicked the Talk button over and over in frustration, then moved into the centre of the basement, where he absent-mindedly picked a hockey stick up off the floor.

"Let's go! The storm is getting worse," the kid's dad called, just as a baby somewhere upstairs started to cry. "Grab your equipment and get in the van!"

The kid paused for a moment, then hooked the walkie-talkie onto his pocket and scooped a puck up onto the blade of his stick. He bounced it once, twice, and then smacked it down onto the cold basement floor.

Is he going to shoot at us?

Bond couldn't believe it.

Mouth Guard's eyes grew wide. He'd moved the net up against them for cover, and now he and Bond were too close to it. Any shot fired at the net would be fired at them, too.

Then he'll find us for sure, thought Bond. *He'll knock our teeth out and we'll get caught.*

With his eyes on the net, the kid drew back his stick.

And then suddenly, just as he was about to fire, an answer came through.

BZZZZ-SHEEEP-ZZZZ!

"We're . . . here! The captain—"

SHEEEP-ZZZZ!

"We're on a boat . . . and we're heading toward the . . . " The voice trailed off.

Caught off guard by the response, the kid stumbled and took a slapshot that veered to the left and missed the net completely. But the shot was so strong, so powerful, that it ricocheted off the clothes dryer and then off a cracked plastic sink before it slammed into a steel support pole, making it ring like a bell.

"Where are you? Where?" the kid asked desperately, throwing down his stick and pulling out the walkie-talkie as fast as he could. "Do you need help?"

"We're coming into . . . *what*? Halifax Harbour. If the waves don't flip us ov . . . over . . . first." The voice was shaky, scared, but also familiar.

How can a scratchy voice on a walkie-talkie feel so . . . like I know him? Bond wondered. But before she could figure it out on her own, she had her answer.

In an instant, Mouth Guard was standing, facing the kid who'd just shot the puck off the dryer, and his mouth was moving.

"That's Lucas!"

CHAPTER 3
Halifax Harbour, Nova Scotia

Lucas couldn't believe his eyes—or his stomach.

He was starting to feel seasick, and he didn't know what to do about it. There was no time for puking.

The waves crashing over the sides of the boat, tossing the small fishing trawler from side to side, were enormous white-capped monsters. But the ones smashing up against the wharf in the harbour ahead of them, jostling the other boats around like they were sticks going over a waterfall, were full-on Godzillas.

"Are we even going to make it back to shore?" Lucas asked the captain nervously. He felt inside his pocket for his lucky quarter—in case luck was something they'd need—and realized he'd forgotten to pack it.

The captain's thick black trench coat and clunky rain boots were still glistening from when he'd snuck around the side of the ship in the blowing rain, bursting through the doorway of his storage room to find three damp hockey players.

At first he'd thought they were stowaways, but Swift had quickly explained that they were desperate to get *off* this ship, not stay *on* it, and he seemed to have believed them.

"Will we make it? Can't be sure, son," the captain answered with his big, gravelly voice. The boat teetered to the port side again with even more force than before, but Captain Horatio Brannen didn't flinch. He said he'd seen far worse out on the water years ago, back when he used to drive a tugboat.

Lucas had been on boats at his grandfather's cottage many times, and he'd never felt sick. His grandfather—he called him Bompa—would ride in the back of the canoe, making large, sweeping strokes, while Lucas rode in the front, trying not to grip his paddle like a hockey stick. It was fun. He loved it.

But *fun* wasn't how this boat ride felt.

This is more like a theme-park ride, Lucas thought. He tried to steady himself as another big rolling wave hit.

"How fast is that wind?" asked Swift, mesmerized by the storm. She leaned in toward a window that was

spotted with spray from the downpour, her eyes as wide as hockey pucks. "This is really amazing."

Swift loved weather of any kind. She loved lightning storms, snow falling on outdoor rinks, and warm, windy summers where she could take out her strawberry-blonde ponytail and let her hair fly around until it ended in knots.

She even loves weather that might kill us, Lucas thought.

"Those winds are probably going 120 kilometres a hour—and that hurricane's not done with us yet," said Captain Brannen, leaning back in his seat. "*Ha*, but nothing can kill me!"

Then why aren't you *the one steering the boat?* Lucas wondered, but he was too timid to say it out loud.

The captain, tired from a long night of steering through bad weather, had handed the wheel to Edge. And Lucas couldn't believe his friend had actually taken it! He'd also taken a compass that the captain had given him—to keep!

Abruptly, Edge steered them toward a wave and slowed so they could take it head-on. The bow of the trawler rose high, seemed to hang there for a moment, and then crashed down again, sending water in all directions. They'd passed two big container ships, and were aiming toward the open water between a large island and the mainland.

Then another wave hit. And another. And suddenly, they were getting close to shore—being pushed through the mouth of the harbour. Lucas could see people running along the Halifax waterfront, trying to fasten their boats with extra safety lines as huge gusts of wind blew rain at them, almost like buckets of water being thrown on their heads. The few trees they could see looked as though their branches were strips of ribbon being tossed around in the wind. And although the sun was now up, everything on shore had turned grey, like a black-and-white photograph where only people's raincoats and the blurry yellow of car headlights had been coloured back in.

Edge struggled to hold the wheel of the boat steady.

"Everything's soaked!" said Swift.

But Lucas already knew that. He'd just finished searching through the bag of supplies he'd packed in Riverton: the portable night light he'd borrowed from his little brother, Connor, and the jackknife he'd tucked into his sock were both dripping wet. Even his beloved journal was soaked through.

Lucas couldn't turn a page without it ripping! On the first page, a tear had already started right down the soggy middle of his drawing of Mario Lemieux posing in his Pittsburgh Penguins jersey. Lucas had carefully put the journal away to protect his other sketches and to give it time to dry out.

Luckily, Crunch's video camera seemed to be fine— at least, the red recording light was still on. Crunch, who'd built a camera into his backpack for recording his bike rides through the woods, had made Lucas trade bags with him just before the leap.

"I'll stay here in case anything goes wrong," Crunch had said. "But that doesn't mean I want to miss out on the adventure. Make sure you RECORD EVERYTHING."

Lucas had nodded even though he'd had no idea where they were headed or what they'd see.

"We're almost there!" Swift now cheered, squinting through the wind and rain.

"*Gnarly-ahoy!*" Edge said excitedly. He looked down at his wrist, wondering if the messages he'd been sending were getting through. Had the kid's walkie-talkie died? Had he been swallowed up by the storm?

Suddenly, Edge's comm-band buzzed again, making all three Ice Chips jump, but the only sound that came through was static.

Just then, Swift let out a yell: "Reverse! Reverse! You're coming in too fast!"

Edge pulled on the handle to reverse the engine. He turned the wheel—hard—and the boat started to skid sideways across the water, carried on one of those rolling waves.

The trawler slowed a little, but it wasn't reversing.

And they were still going way too fast.

Lucas's stomach did a somersault. He'd been watching the waves, not the harbour. And now he really *was* going to puke.

"Pull back, pull back!" Swift shouted. "Go around that big pier!"

She quickly turned to Captain Brannen, who seemed to be brushing a piece of lint off his uniform. He wasn't even watching out the window! *Maybe he really* doesn't *care if the storm kills him?*

"Top Shelf!" Edge said hurriedly, using Lucas's nickname, just as he did when they were on the ice. "We're going to get slammed!"

But Lucas was already one play ahead of him.

"You're offence, I'm defence—we can do this," he shouted as he grabbed his helmet and two large white buoys that were hanging on the wall.

Moving as quickly as he could, Lucas burst through the ship's side door.

"Hold back as much as you can. Once these buoys are on, they'll take the hit!" Lucas yelled as he slipped his helmet over his head to protect himself from the blinding rain.

Edge tried to straighten the boat out as fast as he could, but a wave sprayed up over its side, soaking his best friend. Lucas shook it off as he rushed to tie the two buoys to the side of the boat. His plan: the floaters would soften the blow when the boat hit against the pier—and it was *definitely* going to crash into that pier!

"Okay—get ready!" Swift shouted at Lucas through the storm.

One buoy was on, but he was still fumbling with the other rope.

"You're going to have to turn to port—that's left—*hard*!" Swift yelled frantically toward the helm as she rushed to Edge's side. That's what Coach Small always told them: if you were coming at a player and couldn't stop, it was always better for both players if you turned your shoulder. Captain Brannen probably could have given them some real advice—some boating advice—but for some reason, he wasn't saying a word.

Lucas finally had the rope tied to the buoy and was ready to throw it over the side like he had the first one, but without warning, Edge flipped the handle into reverse—it was too soon! The bow of the boat was now burrowing through the waves so hard that they nearly fishtailed.

Water was flying all over the place: rain and waves everywhere. Lucas lost his balance—and he still hadn't thrown the second buoy over.

But Edge couldn't wait any longer or they'd crash nose first. With Swift's help, he turned the wheel hard to the left to get into position.

It was as though they were moving in slow motion but still didn't have time to think. And then suddenly . . .

THUNK! KA-RACK!

The boat crashed sideways against the side of the pier, just as Lucas had said it should.

With an impressive jolt, it bounced off the spot where the one buoy had been placed and was tossed back into the ocean several feet, sending Lucas and the buoy he hadn't yet secured tumbling overboard!

"LU-CAAAAS!" Swift yelled, running out to the bow of the ship.

Lucas had been standing there only a moment ago. And now all Swift could see was the spray shooting up from the waves beneath them.

"Someone help! LUCAS!" she called frantically, just as two familiar faces, dripping with rain, slowly came into focus on the pier.

CHAPTER 4
Riverton: A Few Days Earlier

Lucas bit down hard, yanked back, and felt his little finger sting as the top of his nail ripped away. He hoped it wouldn't bleed. He knew he'd have to stop—his mother had promised she'd try to scrape together enough money for a better pair of hockey pants if he'd only stop biting his nails—but he couldn't. Not now. Not even long enough to swallow his weekend breakfast of Cheerios, one scrambled egg, and a glass of milk.

This morning, the Ice Chips were playing their very first game at the reopened Riverton Community Arena.

Their rink.

Even if Lucas didn't feel ready, he at least looked it—standing in the sun on the front stoop of his house, waiting beside his equipment.

With the tip of his sneaker, he drew three small rocks out of the garden and lined them up on the concrete slab in front of him. He turned his foot slightly, cradling one of the stones in the curve of his shoe, and aimed at a space between two small shrubs farther down the lawn, away from where his grandfather and brother, Connor, were playing.

Lucas whispered under his breath as he kicked each of the three stones at the bushes, one after another: "WE . . . WILL . . . LOSE!" One goal, two misses.

Lucas had never said that before. He'd never *thought* it before. But after last night's practice, not even Coach Small could deny it: this year's Ice Chips were terrible.

"Play hard, but have fun," Lucas's mom had said, wishing him luck. Then she'd climbed into the car with his father so they could run off and open the Whatsit Shop, leaving Bompa to look after Connor. Lucas had just smiled and shrugged—how could he tell them how unprepared his team was?

This wasn't a real game—not one that counted for the hockey league. But even if it was only for exhibition, mostly to show the town how well the old community rink had been fixed up, it was still a game.

Besides, Lucas *had* to count it: they were playing against the Riverton Stars, the town's only other competitive novice team, and the Stars counted everything.

ROY MacGREGOR AND KERRY MacGREGOR

Last year, Beatrice and Jared Blitz had marked every point against the Chips on the wall of their dressing room at the old rink. But now that their team had moved into the fancy Blitz Sports Complex, built by their dad, they'd probably be counting those points on a Jumbotron!

"You kids will improve—believe me, it'll get better," Bompa said as he rushed past Lucas with a now diaper-less Connor tucked under his arm like a football. Connor was laughing and wiggling, pretending he was going to make a run for it. "And maybe the hockey gods will smile down on you today," Bompa added with a kind chuckle as he pushed open the front door and went inside.

But how can it get better? Lucas wondered. So far, none of their practices had gone well. Bond couldn't shoot, and Mouth Guard couldn't pass. Swift's sister, Sadie—now known as "Blades" to the Chips— was catching on quickly, but Lars Larsson, the bully, wouldn't stop hogging the puck. And then there was Lucas himself . . .

He should have felt better than he did. He was taller and stronger after this summer's growth spurt. But he'd started using one of his cousin Speedy's hand-me-down sticks, which was right for his new height, and he wasn't used to it yet. It was throwing everything off. At least, Lucas hoped that was the problem.

At their last practice, only a few of the players had done okay. Crunch put one in off the crossbar. Edge scored on a sweet deke, and Lars went five-hole. But no one else could score on Swift. Lucas came in, fumbled the puck, then tried to flip it high over Swift's blocker — but it landed low instead. An easy save for her.

The situation was simple: they just weren't ready.

Lucas grabbed another couple of rocks — this time with his hockey stick. Being careful not to let the blade touch the ground, he shot those through the bushes, too. This time, zero for two.

He shifted his chewing to another nail. He couldn't wait for this day to be done. *Where are they?* he wondered, just as his comm-band finally buzzed.

It was Edge.

Buzzed again. It was Swift.

Buzzed again. It was Crunch.

Lucas's teammates were just around the corner.

He took a small sliver of nail from between his teeth and tossed it into the bushes. He quickly retied one of his shoelaces and hoisted his hockey bag up onto his shoulder.

It was time.

A moment later, Edge, Swift, Crunch, and Lucas were all together, working hard to make jokes to get their spirits up.

"We've got this," said Swift with a hopeful smile.

"Yeah, let's kick some butt for that *rock-a-silly* rink of ours," Edge said to Lucas, giving his best friend a little push.

Lucas knew how Edge felt: they owed it to their beloved old rink—the rink that had almost been closed down . . . but now belonged to them, and them alone.

Now we just need to own the ice, too, he thought as he and his teammates set off toward their first pre-season game against the Stars.

✳ ✳ ✳

"What the—?" began Edge. He stopped suddenly, and Crunch walked right into him.

Lucas couldn't say a word.

The four Chips had arrived at the old Riverton rink just in time to see a bus pull up to the front doors.

The bus was brand new, and it had a huge Stars logo on the side.

"No way!" said Mouth Guard, who was just lifting his bag out of the trunk of his parents' car. "They've got their own bus?"

Apparently, they did. The bus sighed to a halt, and the side door whooshed open with a burst of air. The driver hopped out and immediately pulled up the luggage door, revealing a dozen new hockey bags, each with the words "Riverton Stars" and a player's number on it. There were dozens of high-end composite sticks, too.

The Blitz twins bounded down the stairs of the new bus. Beatrice was first. Her new jacket, track pants, and cap were all in the team's colours—maroon, black, and gold—and all read "B. Blitz" and the number 13. Smiling at the twins, the driver reached in and yanked out the top two bags—Beatrice's and then one with a 9, for Jared.

"Do they have to carry their own bags . . . all the way to the *door*?" Bond asked sarcastically, walking up to her new teammates.

The other Stars were now grabbing their bags, too, and heading toward the rink entrance. As they walked past, they paid no attention to the Ice Chips standing to the side, their own bags over their shoulders and their sticks in their hands.

Lucas and Swift stood together, burning as they listened to what Coach Blitz's players were saying.

"They should have torn this old barn down when they had the chance!"

"I'd quit if I still had to play at this rink!"

"This place is a joke!"

"Just like the team that practises here!"

When the Stars had moved on, Swift leaned in and whispered into Lucas's ear: "We'll show them who practises *here*."

Lucas smiled back . . . but of course, that was exactly what he was afraid of.

CHAPTER 5

The Zamboni doors closed. The ice was now glistening and hardening. The Ice Chips stood at one gate, flexing their legs impatiently. The Riverton Stars were at the other gate, their helmets pressed to the glass.

For a meaningless exhibition game, the tension was thick enough to cut with a skate blade.

The doors opened and the kids flooded onto the ice. First was Bond, who started with a quick stutter step—her signature move back when she played roller derby—before she bolted across the fresh, clean surface.

If she could just get a shot to go with that beautiful stride, thought Lucas, *she'd really be amazing.*

Blades, Edge, and Alex Stepanov, the small, Russian-speaking forward who went by "Dynamo," were next. Swift slammed her pads hard once she made it to the crease, and Crunch and Maurice Boudreau, called "Slapper" because of his mean slapshot, bumped gloves over the red line. Then came Lars, who stepped out with his head down and a serious expression on his face, as if he was ready to play the game of his life.

Then, finally, Lucas. He was the last at the boards, as usual.

"Get a move on!" Edge yelled with a laugh in Lucas's direction as he scooped up a puck and fired on Swift. "We need our *Top-inator*, our *Top Shazam*, our *Top Shelf-a-go-go* . . . "

Edge's word babble was often endless, but it made Lucas giggle.

Letting go of some of his nervousness, Lucas smiled back, stepped onto the ice, and—*WHOOO-OOOOOOPS!*—fell flat on his butt!

He tried to stand back up, but this time his skates slid out to each side, pitching him face-forward onto the ice.

Was this for real?

The other kids were pointing and laughing. None of the parents in the stands could figure out what was happening. Swift was the first to skate over to where Lucas was, flat on the ice.

"Whoa! Are you okay?" she asked.

"My edges are gone," Lucas said, puzzled.

With Swift's help, he made it back to the gate, pulled himself through, stood up, and lifted his right skate. He ran his bare thumb over the steel blade—it was as dull as a Popsicle stick.

He checked his left skate—the same.

What's going on here?

Lucas could only assume the obvious: someone had filed the edges off his skates.

But why? And who? And . . . when?

Then he remembered: he'd had to go *back* into the arena's lobby for his pre-game ritual that morning. On his way in, he'd somehow forgotten to kiss his fingers and touch the glass case with the photo of the two boys holding the championship trophy—one of his pre-game superstitions. Half-dressed, he'd hurried back out to the lobby—for only a moment—leaving his skates alone in the dressing room.

Well, not entirely alone. Lars had still been there, getting ready.

Lucas looked out the open gate door. Most of the players on the ice were still staring at him—except Lars, who was skating by with a guilty expression on his face.

Lars wouldn't—would he?

"Go, but go fast," Coach Small said as he gave Lucas a quick pat on the back.

Lucas knew his coach was talking about the sharpener's shop in the lobby—and he knew that he had only a few minutes before the warm-up would end and the game would begin.

Luckily, the skate sharpener was able to get to work right away.

"Looks like someone ground them into the cement floor," Mr. Johansen said sympathetically as he turned on his machine. "Took every bit of the edge right off."

When he finally turned the spinning stone sharpener off again, Mr. Johansen checked the edges with his eye. Then he took a whetstone in his thick hands and rubbed it along the blades of both skates before handing them back to Lucas.

"You're good to go," he said. "Get back out there!"

Lucas still couldn't believe it. He'd already been so concerned about his stickhandling, and now he had to worry about *sabotage*? From one of his own teammates?

"Gotta be the Blitz twins—they're going *down*," Edge said, suddenly appearing beside his best friend.

"Maybe," said Lucas, hurrying into his newly

sharpened skates. But there was no time to talk about Lars or the twins. The game was about to start!

The two Ice Chips made it back to the rink just as the referee was raising his whistle to his lips. A quick wave of tension ran through the arena as the shrill sound echoed off the boards. Lucas hated that feeling, but he loved it, too.

Go time.

He could see that Coach Small had called Bond, Lars, and Mouth Guard over to the bench for a chat that was now breaking up.

The coach nodded and clapped his hands as the three young players moved back onto the ice. "Think ahead out there!" he called. "You hear me, Dylan?"

Mouth Guard nodded back, blushing as he realized he was being singled out, but fully aware that he deserved it. Passing was the weakest part of his game, and he hadn't been able to hide that from anyone — not even the bully Lars, who was smirking as he made his way toward the bench to wait his turn.

Fweee-uuurllll!

The referee whistled to make sure the players were in their positions.

Lucas was happy to feel his edges catch as he stepped

back onto the ice and hurried to get to his spot as centre. At the blue line, he turned to skate backwards so he could admire the long bracket marks his razor-sharp skates left in the fresh ice. If he were an artist, this would be his masterpiece.

Of course, right now Lucas was more concerned with being an athlete—even just an average one. If he could think like a hockey player again—if *all* the Ice Chips could, just for this one game!—maybe their season wouldn't start out as a total disaster.

CHAPTER 6

The referee and linesmen took up their positions, and the ref whistled for a player from each team to come to centre ice. Lucas skated over slowly, making sure he tapped his stick on the pads of his linemates, Mouth Guard and Edge, as he passed.

He coasted nervously to the faceoff dot, then looked up to see Beatrice Blitz skating toward him, a sneer on her face.

"How're your skates, loser?" Beatrice asked.

Lucas burned red. *Is she the one who put Lars up to it?*

He looked around for some kind of sign that the hockey gods might be on the Ice Chips' side, as his bompa had said—but nothing. That is, until the Stars' goalie banged his stick against his pads . . .

Before Lucas had stepped onto the ice—before falling on his butt—he'd made sure to check out the other team's players, especially their goalie. He'd noticed that the kid had a good glove hand and liked to flick it out with great drama. He'd also noticed that the goalie liked to go down early, sliding on his big pads across the crease to ensure no one could slip a puck through his five-hole.

That had given Lucas an idea. If he got a chance, he'd try it.

All eyes were on Lucas, Beatrice, and the small black disc in the referee's hands.

And then all of a sudden, the puck was thrown down and the game was on.

Beatrice won the draw and sent the puck back to one of her defencemen, who came up fast through the middle and dropped the puck just before hitting the Chips' blue line. Jared Blitz picked it up, slipped right between Crunch and Bond, faked a shot that Swift went for, and easily drove it into the Chips' net.

It was 1–0, and Lucas hadn't even touched the puck!

As Lucas's line was called in and Lars's line took its place, Blades skated by Lucas.

"I'm surprised the Stars didn't bring an anthem singer," she said, making him laugh.

She was right: Coach Small was alone at their bench,

wearing a bulky sweater and his old grey cap. But at the Stars' bench, Coach Blitz was all dressed up with some fancy assistant beside him. The two men looked almost identical in new caps, team jackets, shirts, and ties.

Lucas shook his head. *What, do they think they're in the NHL?*

Throughout the period, Lucas's line was back on the ice and then off again, but nothing seemed to improve. At the end of it, the Stars were ahead 4–0.

"We're going to try a change," Coach Small said, tapping Lucas on the arm. "You trade places with Lars."

Lucas understood that lines sometimes get changed around. And he knew that Lars had played well, while he'd been having trouble. But to lose his spot to that bully was like having his heart yanked out of his chest!

Was this Lars's plan all along?

For the second period, Lucas played on a line with Blades and Dynamo. The Stars were up 7–0, but Lucas caught a long pass from Blades and found himself on a breakaway.

He came in hard over the other team's blue line, looked up, and saw the Stars' goalie flick his catching glove like a lobster about to grab something juicy. Lucas knew he wouldn't be trying a shot there.

ROY MacGREGOR AND KERRY MacGREGOR

Instead, he slipped to the side, looping in on the net from the right and skating hard across the front of the crease.

As expected, the Stars' goalie went down on his knees, ready to block any backhand that Lucas might try.

But Lucas had other ideas.

Instead of shooting, he let the puck slide and fall back between his skate blades. He then reached his stick back with one hand and tapped the puck. It slid into the net as slow as a curling stone landing on the button.

The referee's whistle blew—Lucas had scored!

And now he was piling into the boards!

Lucas never saw what happened; he just felt it. A stick was between his legs and suddenly he was down, sliding hard into the end boards. He spun as he fell, his back taking the blow while he watched the Stars' number 13 skate away, laughing.

The whistle went again—a penalty to Beatrice Blitz.

* * *

The Chips started the third period on a power play because of Beatrice's penalty—their first of the game.

Coach Small sent out Edge, Mouth Guard, and Crunch, then tapped Lucas again.

"Your line's up. Play the point with Bond, okay?" Coach Small said.

Lucas jumped over the boards, not even bothering with the gate. The coach was showing faith in him again. He felt his heart swell. He was back on his line!

With Beatrice out, the Chips had one more skater on the ice than the Stars—"the man advantage," as they called it in the pros—and Lucas knew that an extra player could make a big difference.

Edge won the faceoff and shot the puck up-ice, with Mouth Guard chasing hard and reaching it just before it went over the icing line. While trying to get the pass back to Lucas, however, Mouth Guard fumbled it. The puck was easily picked up by Jared Blitz, who fired it high along the boards to get it out of the Stars' end.

Only, it didn't get out. Bond, gliding out of her zone, chopped the puck right out of the air. Nervously, she took her shot, but it was weak and fluttered, and a Stars' defenceman blocked it with his shin pads. It then rebounded over to Edge, who stickhandled it back in behind the Stars' net.

No one was covering Edge, the extra man, so Lucas pinched in from the blue line, driving hard to the net. Edge fed him the puck, and Lucas fired to the blocker side—but the puck rang off the crossbar and rebounded high over the Plexiglas!

So close, so close. Lucas swore if he got another chance, he'd fire the puck along the ice.

Next, Mouth Guard took the faceoff against the Stars' other forward—a new, big guy whose name Lucas didn't know—and was beaten cleanly. The player swept the puck to Jared, who again fired it hard around the boards.

The puck was in the air, and Lucas managed to knock it down with his stick.

Bond, the only player not covered this time, advanced out of her zone again, pinching hard toward the Stars' net. She slammed her stick twice on the ice to let her teammate know she wanted the puck.

Lucas fired his pass to Bond, but Jared Blitz beat her to it—just as Beatrice bounded back onto the ice.

The Chips' power play was over.

It was now a two-on-one in the Chips' end, with only Lucas back—and he wasn't a defenceman.

The only Chip within range was Edge, but he was

behind the twins and coming in on the wrong side.

Beatrice, who now had the puck, skated toward Lucas. He tried to poke-check her, but she faked left and niftily sent the puck over to her twin, who had a clear path to the net.

Jared roared in on Swift, and just as she thought she had him, he slid the puck back to his sister, who roofed it high into the net.

Stars 8, Chips 1.

Gliding past Lucas with her stick in the air, Beatrice cackled. Slowly, she raised her gloved index finger and marked a point in the air.

A disaster, just as Lucas had feared.

CHAPTER 7

No one spoke in the dressing room. The Ice Chips slowly took off their equipment, sighing and groaning. Coach Small came in shaking his head, but he said nothing.

Finally, someone broke the silence. No surprise that it was Mouth Guard.

Lucas saw it coming the moment his teammate stripped off his sweaty T-shirt and slipped his hand in under his armpit.

PPPPFFFFWWWWHHHHHHEEEEEEEE-EEEEEEET!!!!!

This was Mouth Guard's new thing: *throwing farts*—the same way a ventriloquist with a dummy on his lap throws his voice. He'd just made it sound as though the fart had come from the rusty bathroom stall beside their dressing room door.

Some of the Chips giggled, unable to help them-selves. But Lucas didn't.

He knew it was a fake fart, but he also knew that the Ice Chips stunk. For real.

Lucas wanted to believe that the hockey gods had been *against* them this game, but really he knew that the Chips just hadn't played well enough. They needed practice. And they needed help. Everyone on the ice knew it, and so did everyone in the stands.

Mouth Guard had tried his best to make good passes out there, but they always seemed to fall *behind* the moving player, the same way they had during prac-tice. The guy could shoot, but he couldn't direct the puck unless he was aiming at a net—one of the few things on the ice that didn't move.

And Bond's stickhandling problems were even worse than before. The one time Mouth Guard *did* get a proper pass to her, moving in from the blue line, she'd whiffed on her shot completely and fallen down, slid-ing helplessly into the corner. Jared and Beatrice had both laughed so hard they'd turned red. Coach Blitz and his fancy new assistant had cracked smiles, too!

The Chips were jokes out on the ice—ridiculous clowns with blades strapped to their feet and zero abil-ity to protect their net.

Of course, Lucas was one of those clowns. Coach Small, who never yelled but was never really able to hide his emotions, had clearly grown impatient with Lucas on the ice. He'd lost confidence in him.

Why else did he give Lars my position?

Lucas knew that if he didn't step up his game, he could lose that position permanently.

"Listen up!" Coach Small called as Mouth Guard finished off another big fart—this time making it come from the metal garbage can in the corner of the room. "Look, guys, we missed some practice time while the rink was being repaired at the beginning of the season. We're rusty. We *all* know that."

A few of the players nodded.

"This was just an exhibition game, but it counted all the same because it was a test," Coach Small continued carefully, clearing his throat. "A test of where we stand this year against the Stars."

"Where we stand? You mean where we fall on our faces," Bond said, half laughing, half trying not to cry.

Lucas nodded in her direction, wishing he could make her feel better. Swift, who was standing beside Bond, quietly linked arms with her.

"Yeah, what *happened* out there?" Lars asked

loudly from one of the benches along the far wall. He glared at Mouth Guard, then at Bond. "You gotta be able to play better than *that*."

"We *will* play better," Edge said, shooting the exact same glare back at Lars.

Coach Small ignored the looks flying around the dressing room and went back to his speech. "I just don't want you to forget that while we might not have the Stars' fancy rink or their expensive uniforms, we have something even better—something that can't be bought. We have *heart*." As the coach said this, he thumped his fist proudly in the centre of his chest. "I want to see your *heart* at our next practice, regardless of what happened out there today. Understand?"

"HEART!" Swift repeated, unlinking her arm with Bond's so she could smack her goalie stick against the metal garbage can.

"Heart!" Edge yelled, thumping his chest twice.

"Heart!" others called.

Some pounded their sticks on the rubber flooring. Others clapped.

Lucas tapped his stick along with them, but he couldn't bring himself to shout.

How can you yell "Heart!" when you're heartbroken?

And how can you say you love your team when you're dragging it down?

* * *

On Sunday night, a few of the Ice Chips met in Bond's driveway. They'd set up a Shooter Tutor—a rubberized canvas guide—across the front of an old hockey net. They took turns trying to fire the puck through the five different holes that marked the best places to score.

Lucas wasn't the only one struggling after yesterday's loss. Coach Small had made it clear to everyone that if they wanted to feel better, they'd have to improve.

Edge had little trouble and hit all five holes in under ten tries. Mouth Guard hit five in twelve tries. Lucas was five in fifteen—way worse than last year. And Bond only managed to hit the three bottom holes after about twenty tries. She couldn't hoist the puck at all.

"Can we . . . *help*?" Edge asked, smiling and leaning on his stick. He didn't want to offend Bond, but if he could do something to make this easier for her, he would.

"Well . . . " Bond started, sounding unsure. "How do I lift it up? Is it the angle of the stick or something?"

"Kind of," Lucas said as he scooped up a ball for a quick wrist shot that didn't make it in. He knew how to lift a puck off the ground—knew when it felt right—but he'd never actually tried to explain it to anyone.

"I'm also afraid someone will steal the puck from me. I don't really like that part of the game," Bond said as she carefully lined up another shot. "Stand back, okay?"

Swift hadn't come out because she needed to work on her hurdles for track, but with the Shooter Tutor, Bond could practise her shot anyway. A few of the Chips had gone to the Riverton shopping mall that morning to get it with Bond's dad—who, they'd learned, had his own wild sports story.

* * *

Lucas, Bond, and Mouth Guard had just jumped out of Bond's parents' truck in the mall parking lot when Mr. Foster told them about his time on the Jamaican bobsled team.

"No way!" Lucas shouted, right before Mouth Guard launched into a thousand and one questions.

Bond's dad said that while he was taking part in a Jamaican push-cart derby—a race with small wooden go-karts—he'd met two Americans who were putting together a bobsled team. The Americans were searching all over Jamaica for athletes, and when they finally had a team together and trained, they'd sent it to the 1988 Winter Olympics in Calgary.

"The whole world loved the team," Bond said as the mall's automatic doors slid open in front of them. "Even though they didn't win a medal."

"It's amazing that they made it so far!" Lucas said, smiling as they walked toward the mall's glassed-in elevator.

There was only enough room for the three Chips, an old man with a cane, and a young mother with a baby in a stroller, so the kids all crammed in while Mr. Foster bounded up the stairs toward the sports store on the second floor.

"The team was amazing—but my dad wasn't in that bobsled," Bond said, sadly. "He quit before the big competition, and another bobsledder took his place."

Neither of her teammates asked why her dad had quit—they were happy enough to be hanging out at the mall with an almost-Olympic athlete!

"Does your dad talk a lot about their training? How did they do it without any snow around?" Lucas asked as the elevator doors closed.

"Yeah, sometimes they had to—" Bond started, but Mouth Guard, unable to focus as usual, had just slipped his hand through the neck hole of his T-shirt.

PPPPFFFFWWWWHHHHHHEEEEEEEEEEE-EEEET!!!!!

Lucas rolled his eyes, but Bond could barely keep down her giggles.

PPFFFFHHWEEET! PPFFFFHHWEEET! PPFFFFH-HWEEET!

Mouth Guard snapped his arm down over his hand like a chicken wing, making the most disgusting sound imaginable.

Lucas knew his face had to be beet red. There were tears squeezing out of his eyes, he was fighting so hard not to burst out laughing.

Then Mouth Guard let out two little squeaky ones—Connor-sized toots—and Lucas knew he would lose it. He was killing them!

PPFFFFHHWEEET!

PPFFFFHHWEEET!

Mouth Guard sniffed the air suspiciously and looked quickly at the old man, who was staring so hard at the floor numbers that he might not even have heard the revolting sounds.

As the door opened at the second floor, Mouth Guard, dramatically holding his nose, jumped free, followed by a giggling Bond and Lucas—both of them also holding their noses.

The doors closed and the glass-walled elevator continued its rise. The Chips gathered by the railing, staring up and laughing hysterically as they noticed the young mother, still standing behind the old man.

She was holding her nose, too!

"You are *awful*!" Bond laughed, leaning over with her hands on her knees, trying to breathe.

"Stop!" Lucas cried as he wiped tears of laughter from his cheeks.

That's when another noise suddenly burst through the group, grabbing everyone's attention.

BUZZZZZZZZ!

Lucas's comm-band was buzzing—it was Crunch.

And it was a call that would change everything.

❖   ❖   ❖

With Lucas, Edge, and Mouth Guard now standing on the road beside the driveway, Bond took another shot at the Shooter Tutor. This one lifted a little, but it struck the garage door behind the net—it wasn't even close.

"You'll get it," Lucas called, trying to be encouraging. He would have said more, but he could see that Bond didn't want to hear it.

Crunch, he knew, had already said too much. He'd made that desperate call to Lucas's comm-band at the mall, and when Lucas answered, Crunch had delivered the news that sent shivers down the spine of every Ice Chip: "*The Stars are challenging us to a rematch!*"

Bond's shoulders had slumped immediately, but they'd still met up with her dad in the sports store and bought the Shooter Tutor anyway.

Now, they just wished they had more time to use it.

"Aren't the *losers* supposed to be the ones who ask for a rematch?" Bond asked, throwing a hand on her hip after missing another shot. "We're not ready! At least, *I'm* not."

"You really think they'll beat us again?" Mouth Guard asked, picking up Bond's rebound. He tried to pass it to Edge, who was moving in front of the net, but he shot it too far behind him. Another miss.

"Will they beat us? What do *you* think?" said Lucas, not even reaching for the ball as it rolled down the driveway.

CHAPTER 8

The moment Lucas stepped into the Riverton Community Arena, the smell of hockey filled his nostrils. Quiet Dave the Iceman—the man who'd made Lucas promise never to break into the rink again—had completely resurfaced the ice for last Saturday's game. And although Lucas hated the memory of that embarrassing loss to the Stars, he still loved the smell of Dave's cleaning products.

There weren't many pleasures in the world that Lucas cared for as much as those first few steps into a hockey rink: the smell of cement floors freshly cleaned and swept; the motion of the Zamboni making its final circle of the ice; and soon, the feel of the fresh, cold ice itself. *That* was Lucas's paradise.

"You made it! Finally!" Crunch called out as he grabbed Lucas's backpack off his shoulder and started running with it toward the dressing room.

"You could've taken the heavy one!" Lucas called, letting out an excited giggle as he shifted his hockey bag to the other shoulder and picked up his pace.

We should have two hours, easy, to pull this off, he thought. That's at least how long the parents' welcome dinner at the mayor's house would last tonight. All the Chips' parents had been invited, and Coach Small and Quiet Dave would be there, too.

On this night—the night before the big rematch—Lucas and his friends would be the only ones at the rink.

"Top *Sheeeeeeeeeeeeeelf*! Let's go!" he could hear Edge calling from the dressing room. Swift would be there, of course. She had to be—without her dad's keys, they wouldn't have been able to sneak into the building!

It was in the dressing room, after their final practice last night—the worst practice Lucas had had in his life—that Edge had come up with this plan.

"We do know *one way* to get more practice time," he'd whispered into Lucas's ear as he'd unstrapped his second shin pad.

"No, absolutely not—*we can't*!" Lucas had replied, a little too loudly, while zipping up his hockey bag. Then he lowered his voice. "Edge, you know we *can't*. We promised."

But that's when Swift leaned in, too. "Lucas, I thought you'd do anything for this team. If you want to get used to that longer stick in time for the rematch on Saturday, we're going to *have to* leap again."

They'd still travelled through time only once—the day of the final skate, when they'd done it by accident. They'd thought about leaping a second time after the end of this year's tryouts, but they hadn't done it. Quiet Dave the Iceman was always around, watching them. And in fact, Lucas was a little relieved—he never liked going back on a promise.

Tonight is the first night that Quiet Dave's been gone, Lucas thought as he followed the others out of the dressing room. *And now look at what we're about to do!*

Lucas, Edge, and Swift were all in full equipment, but none of them stepped through the gate. No one dared to touch that perfect shining surface—not until the magical flood was done.

Scratch, the tractor-like flooding machine Crunch had discovered before their first leap through time, was still making circles around the ice as Lucas pressed his helmet up against the Plexiglas above the boards. He was grinning, mesmerized.

Maybe this really is a good idea—or even a great one!

It was still a mystery how Scratch was able to make such a beautiful, almost silky sheet of ice. And the fact that it opened some kind of portal that led to another place and time was . . . well, *ridiculous*. But how else could they describe what had happened?

Skating after Scratch's flood, the three of them knew, was like learning that their team had made the NHL playoffs, or that one of them had won the Hart Memorial Trophy. Skating on it made them feel special—*chosen*, almost—even though Quiet Dave had warned them it was dangerous.

"How do we know it will work again?" Lucas's voice was almost a whisper.

Edge wasn't sure if his friend was talking to him or the hockey gods, but he decided to answer anyway. "If it doesn't work . . . well, at least Quiet Dave will be happy that we can't leap through—"

"It's gotta work!" Crunch cried as he came running over from the stands. He wasn't in his hockey gear, but in full Crunchy mode: his glasses were perched crookedly on his head, he had his tablet under his arm, and he'd been pacing around, mumbling to himself.

"Are you ready for this, Crunch?" Swift asked with a slight curl in her lips.

Lucas, Swift, and Edge were excited to go back in time, but Crunch was ecstatic. He was determined to measure, record, and analyze this jump—to try to understand it.

"I've made a table where I can collect all the quantitative data that we—" Crunch started to say, but instantly, Lucas's and Swift's eyes glazed over.

"Of course you have," Swift said, smiling as Scratch, now finished, rolled off his shimmering ice surface and into the Zamboni chute, where the gates closed behind him.

"It's time!" Edge said eagerly, clapping his gloves together.

Lucas was nodding with a big grin on his face as Crunch tossed the camera-equipped backpack to him.

"Are *you* ready?" Crunch asked Swift, teasing.

"One hundred and fifty percent," she said, stepping up to the gap in the boards.

She was the first to push off onto the perfect ice surface.

Then Edge.

Then Lucas.

Swift always started with her prosthetic leg—an old habit, to test that it was working right. While playing,

she never favoured that leg—the one she'd had to have replaced below the knee when she was five—but when you play a game like hockey, some rituals are hard to get rid of.

How could we not have come back here? Look at this ice! Lucas thought with amazement as the three Chips stopped in front of the goalie crease.

Soon, they were all holding hands and gliding as one. They had their eyes on the blue line . . . then on the red. They were moving fast. And they were focused, excited, and afraid—all at the same time.

That's probably why they didn't notice when the door in the boards opened again . . . and Bond and Mouth Guard, also fully dressed, stepped onto the perfect ice surface and began skating toward them.

"Don't forget to—" everyone could hear Crunch yelling as Lucas, Edge, and Swift hit the centre line at the same time and then . . . *poof*.

They were gone.

CHAPTER 9
Halifax Harbour, Nova Scotia

"*NOOOOOOOOOOO!*"

Bond couldn't believe what she was seeing. She and Mouth Guard had *finally* found the boat they were looking for, and now it was careening dangerously in the white-capped waves, coming in hard and fast toward the harbour!

It was out of control. And it was headed straight toward them!

They'd been so lucky up until now: the kid had figured out where the Ice Chips' boat must be with the help of his walkie-talkie, then they'd found the right end of the harbour and the right pier—all without Crunch's tablet or comm-bands or anything!

Bond and Mouth Guard had made their way through the storm—and they were finally *here*!

But were they too late?! Had they arrived only in

time to watch their friends crash and sink to the bottom of the harbour?

Just as they were running along the pier, waving and shouting, the boat pitched sideways—it seemed to leap out of the water. It turned—with Lucas, soaked, holding on to the railing at the front—and skidded dangerously across the water.

There wasn't any time to think, to yell, to get help . . .

And then the boat, with Lucas clinging on desperately, crashed sideways into the pier with a loud crack!

"Lucas!" Bond and Mouth Guard both yelled, shocked, as the boat rebounded with enormous force, sending their friend tumbling overboard into the violent, rising water!

We can't lose him now!

The thought hit Bond like a lightning bolt: *How will we get home without him?*

"*Top Sheeeelf!!*" she yelled over the edge of the pier, squinting down at the crashing, churning waves. She'd been out in the rain for only a moment, but already she was dripping. "Lucas! Where are you? LUCAS! *LUCAS!!*"

On the boat, Swift was yelling, too.

Mouth Guard, however, was just staring at the white-capped waves, his mouth wide open.

He was the one who'd convinced the kid—Sid—to get his parents to drive them from their home in Cole Harbour to Halifax. Sid's parents had seemed a little suspicious at first, but with a hurricane on its way, they weren't about to let two kids run off on their own. Mouth Guard had lied—he'd said that he and Bond were meeting their mom and dad on a boat in the harbour. He'd talked and talked, and somehow he'd managed to sound convincing.

Luckily, Sid's family was already headed to Halifax: Sid had a meeting with some hockey scouts. They were really just higher-level coaches looking for up-and-comers to recruit in the future, his dad had explained, but the Chips could tell it was a big deal for a kid Sid's age to be invited to the scrimmage.

Sid was probably only nine years old, and already coaches were coming to check him out? *Wow! No one wants to see* us *play,* Mouth Guard thought to himself, not realizing the words were also coming out of his mouth.

"*I'd* like to see you play," Sid had said with a smile.

Just before they all squeezed into the family's van, Sid's mom had to run upstairs with his sister, Taylor, to change the baby's diaper one last time, so Sid handed Mouth Guard his stick and puck to take some shots on the basement net.

Mouth Guard made a few quick, precise goals, but Bond's shot hit the bar and the basement wall, and then rebounded off Sid's parents' dryer—leaving a horrible black dent—before landing in an old snow boot. Mouth Guard had never had trouble firing on a net, but Bond obviously still needed practice. Luckily, though, her shot had solved another problem: if the two Ice Chips were going to travel, they'd need something to wear on their feet.

Sid's parents were slightly nervous as they drove the two Ice Chips—each dressed in a pair of Sid's old boots—to Halifax Harbour, where they'd said their parents would be waiting at their boat. The harbour wasn't far from the big arena where Sid was hoping to impress the coaches, but the road there had been tough—trees down, electrical poles lying on the road, and emergency workers trying to get through.

Bond and Mouth Guard were lucky to have made it so far, so quickly.

But they weren't there just yet . . .

"Lucas! CAN YOU HEAR ME?!" Bond yelled,

waving the hockey stick she was holding as Swift ran for shelter on the boat. Bond and Mouth Guard were still in the van when they'd spotted the boat and had taken off running. She had no idea why she'd brought her stick with her.

"He probably *can't* hear you!" Mouth Guard sputtered, coming back to life. "We need something to throw into the water! Something bright—a lifeguard thing, whatever they're called!"

That's when Swift reappeared on the bow of the boat. She was soaked, terrified, and carrying two bright orange life jackets like the one Lucas was wearing, bound together with a long white rope. Her shouts sounded distant, as though they were coming from the other side of a canyon. "Ready?!" was all Bond and Mouth Guard could make out.

Bond gave Swift a nod and laid down her stick. She grabbed on to the edge of the pier so she could get as close to the water as possible.

Mouth Guard quickly dropped onto his stomach beside her. "He's wearing a life jacket, right? I don't see any orange in the water!"

"He *has to* be in the water!" Bond shouted back, desperate.

"*Noooo! I . . . don't! I'm not . . .*"

Bond could hear the words, but only faintly—and with a strange echo. She wasn't even sure they were words at all, except that she could tell Swift had heard them, too.

The fishing trawler was close enough now to dock safely, but Bond could see that Edge was hanging back. He was waiting so he didn't run Lucas over.

"*I'm down here!*"

Bond and Swift exchanged looks. This time, they were both sure—*it was Lucas!*

Swift was the first to spot him. Bond had to grip the edge of the pier tightly so she could look straight down to where Swift was pointing.

Lucas was there!

Their teammate had fallen over the side of the boat, but then he'd been carried by a wave that had crashed into the pier—a pier with long vertical slats of wood running along it like train tracks. That's what Lucas was clinging to. A mass of fish netting had also washed up against the long boards, and both he and the pier were now caught in it. Lucas looked soaked and desperate— like a wet fly trapped in a bright green spider web.

Luckily, the netting seemed to be helping him hold on—just inches above the rising, heaving waters.

"Lucas? LUCAS!" Bond yelled, motioning for Swift to throw her roped life jackets to him.

Swift nodded and launched the tied jackets over the side of the boat, but she hadn't let out enough rope. She let out more and tried again—and again. But because of the wind, she just couldn't get it to him.

You need a paddle—something hard, Lucas was thinking, looking up toward the underbelly of the trawler.

The waves were rocking Lucas, splashing and taunting him . . . and slowly loosening his grip. He knew he had to try harder—he'd have to escape the net if they were ever going to get him out of the water. Carefully, he reached into the top of his sock and pulled out the jackknife he'd hidden there earlier.

Between waves, Lucas sliced the net in three different spots: one near his hip and two near his ankles. Then he started to wiggle . . .

He kicked his feet out and turned as he often did on a breakaway—with one leg bent, the other one out. He was desperate to get free—and it was working! Parts of the net started to loosen, and then suddenly, the last piece holding him snapped . . .

And Lucas was falling again!

"Wahhhhh!" he screamed, his arms and legs flailing. He reached out, but only grabbed air. He reached farther and felt wetness—the crest of a wave—then something *hard*!

He was terrified at what it could be. A shark? A piece of debris? The pier, crumbling in the hurricane? But a second later, he was being lifted up and pulled from the water . . .

Even through his fear, Lucas snorted when he realized what he'd grabbed: one of the objects he knew best in the world.

A hockey stick!

Some kid Lucas had never seen before was holding Bond's stick, dangling it off the edge of the pier, and now Lucas was clinging to it—for his life.

"Hold on!! HOLD ON, Lucas!" Bond was yelling as she and Mouth Guard wrapped their arms tightly around the kid's waist.

Lucas's equipment was waterlogged—he weighed a ton. But they were determined to reel him in.

"Uuuuugh!!!" Bond, Mouth Guard, and Sid all groaned together. Then with one big heave, Lucas was up and over the side of the pier.

"Thank you—*uhh-huhhhhh. Bletch.* Thank . . . you!"

Lucas sputtered as he rolled onto his side and let the water trapped inside his equipment spill out onto the pier. He was out of breath and exhausted, but he was on shore.

"You . . . okay?" Bond asked, unsure of what they should do next. Take shelter from the storm, probably. But where?

"That was incredible!" cheered Mouth Guard. He and Sid helped Lucas sit up and then stand, while Edge finally, slowly, brought the boat into the pier. Captain Brannen was still unwilling to take the helm, but at least now he was offering some docking instructions.

Lucas looked at Bond, at Mouth Guard, and then at the new kid. "You saved my life," he said, still overwhelmed.

The boy shrugged, embarrassed, and rebuttoned the top of his raincoat. Then with a chuckle, he said, "I've done a lot of fishing, but I've never reeled in a hockey player before. You okay?"

Lucas's cheeks flushed red as the kid reached out his hand.

"Hi, I'm Sid."

CHAPTER 10

"There's *no way* they'll let you do it!" Bond was hurrying along beside Sid, gripping her stick and shaking her head. "I mean, really—are you ridiculous? There's a *hurricane*!"

The Chips were following Sid back to his parents' van, but they knew there wouldn't be enough room for all of them. Plus, they were wet—especially Lucas, who was still dripping like a lobster freshly pulled from the ocean.

Sid had told them to follow him anyway—he said he had a plan.

"They'll say yes, just watch." Sid grinned back at Bond. He was talking about running up Citadel Hill—a long, steep mound of grass just a few blocks away. "My mom and dad know I need to warm up before the scrimmage. If I feel good during training, I always feel good on the ice."

"What kind of . . . *training* are we talking about?" asked Edge, whose arms were still sore from steering the boat through the waves.

"It's *running*, Edge," Mouth Guard said with a friendly smirk. "And it's just a *hill*. How tough can it be?"

Before Swift and Edge stepped off the boat, Sid had asked the Chips what they were doing in the harbour, and Lucas, still dazed, had blabbed that they'd come to Halifax to practise their hockey skills. They were lucky he hadn't said anything about Scratch or their magical ice surface—or how they'd *really* ended up in the harbour. Mouth Guard, of course, was ready to talk, too, but Bond had moved fast and clamped her hand over his mouth.

"*You* have some *serious* explaining to do," she'd whispered to Lucas—her hand still sealing Mouth Guard's lips.

That's when the wind had suddenly lightened and grown warmer. It seemed as though the rain might stop for good. Swift wasn't sure if this was the calm before the storm—a pause before the wind-whipping, house-destroying hurricane they'd been warned about finally made landfall—or if the storm had already passed over them.

As the rain around them changed to a light sprinkle, the other boaters in the harbour had started to relax a bit. They tied off the last of their safety lines, and began to shake out their raincoats and umbrellas. Keeping an eye on the skies, they soon made their way to their cars and the shelter of nearby restaurants. The Chips hadn't seen Captain Brannen leave, but they guessed he'd probably decided to move his boat farther into the harbour.

"We can all train together, Lucas! It'll be awesome!" Sid called excitedly as he leaped over a large puddle and landed beside the van. He was pointing up the street, past the arena where he'd be skating in a couple of hours, to where a big white clock tower sat nestled in the side of a grassy mound.

Sid's dad had one eyebrow raised as he rolled down his rain-spattered window. "It's nice to finally meet your *parents*," he said, looking past his son. The eyebrow was for Mouth Guard and Bond—and the three wet hockey players who were now trailing behind them.

"Oh, yeah, we—" Mouth Guard started to say as the Chips gathered around the van. "They're...uh, not our—"

"We get it. They're not your parents," Sid's mom

said, laughing, just as baby Taylor started giggling in the back seat. Then, with a forgiving smile, she added: "We know how teammates feel like family."

Sid's parents had no idea that Lucas had fallen overboard—nor had they seen him rescued from the water. It was all so embarrassing. Lucas smiled politely and then looked away, hoping they wouldn't ask him why he was the wetter than everyone else—or why he smelled so fishy.

Luckily, the new kid had already moved on to the next challenge.

"So I was thinking—can we run up the hill?" Sid asked, leaning in the window and making a funny face at his sister. "There's time before the skate."

Edge didn't want to think about training, and neither did Swift. They wanted to find out how Bond and Mouth Guard had ended up on the pier: where they'd come from and how they'd made it here from Riverton. But with Sid around—this kid who was now on a mission to train with the Chips, thanks to Lucas—they knew those answers would have to wait.

Sid's dad looked over at his wife, and then they both agreed: the kids could run up the hill, but they'd meet them at the top with the van in case the storm got worse again.

"Yesss! You guys ready?" Sid asked as he spun around and flashed the Chips a giant grin.

"Yeah, I'm in," cheered Swift, with as much enthusiasm as she could manage. She didn't want to say anything, but she knew it was possible that the storm wasn't done with them. *At least at top of the hill, I'll have a better view*, she thought.

"Okay, one run," Lucas agreed reluctantly.

"One run," Sid echoed. His legs were already twitching.

"But wait—where do we leave our stuff while we're running?" Bond asked, tapping the end of her stick a little too hard on Lucas's dripping helmet.

"Throw it in the trunk with mine," Sid said. "Oh, all except *you*." He waved toward Swift, who had her stick tucked under her arm and was wringing the water from her ponytail.

"*Me*—why?" asked Swift, shaking out her hands, confused.

"It's a superstition. I know it's silly—*I'm sorry*," Sid said shyly. "I just never put my stick next to a goalie stick—bad luck. But you can put yours in the back beside Taylor—she *loves* goalies."

Leave our stuff? Lucas thought, remembering what Crunch had told them: keep the backpack on and

RECORD EVERYTHING! He looked meaningfully at Edge, then glanced down at the camera hole in his backpack and back up at Edge again.

"Sure, okay, we'll run . . . " Edge blurted awkwardly. "But Lucas needs his bag—his backpack is . . . *karma-tastical.*" His acting, as always, was terrible, and his eyes were shifting around like the ones in a painting in a haunted mansion. "You know . . . superstitions. He needs his pack or he'll completely lose it!"

How could anyone believe this guy? Lucas wondered, trying not to laugh.

"Yeah, Lucas *always* has his backpack on when he trains," Bond said, covering for them—even if she wasn't sure why. All she knew was that she wanted to hear more of the story . . . and Lucas, Edge, and Swift were the only ones who could tell it.

The Chips tossed the rest of their gear in the trunk. And a moment later, they were racing flat out down the street, leaping over puddles and fallen tree branches, climbing up stairs, and dodging bike racks, as though they were running an urban obstacle course.

"Let's *crush* this hill!" Mouth Guard cheered as he grabbed on to a railing and launched himself up a set of concrete steps.

Edge pushed hard with his legs, trying to catch up to Swift, but she was already at the head of the pack—keeping pace with Sid. Behind Edge was Mouth Guard, followed by Lucas and Bond.

"You *owe* me," Bond hissed into Lucas's shoulder as she pumped her arms hard. "After this run, you tell us *everything*!"

* * *

"Higher! Lift your knees HIGHER!"

Lucas was nearly on the ground, he was laughing so hard. Sid was putting the Chips through his regular training routine—running them up the hill and giving them little exercises along the way—but with all the rain that had fallen, it had turned into more of a grass-stained mud run.

"I can't, I can't!" Bond protested, laughing as she wiped a muddy hand across her forehead. She was trying to lift her knees to her chest as she jogged, but she kept losing her footing—just like the rest of her teammates.

Swift, an experienced runner, was having the most success, but she, too, was out of breath.

Sid was making polite suggestions as he did the

moves along with them, but Edge was repeating every instruction like he was a military drill sergeant.

"Now five twists!" Sid said, giggling because he knew what was coming.

"He said twist!" Edge yelled. "HE SAAAAAAID TWIST!"

The Chips lifted their right legs and twisted them to the left, while twisting their arms to the right. But Mouth Guard slipped on the fourth lift and took out the only leg Lucas was standing on. Lucas tumbled on top of Mouth Guard, making him cry out and sending a spray of mud across the front of Swift's jersey.

Bond rolled her eyes, but Swift just laughed: they'd taken a leap into the past for some training time, and even in this awful weather, it seemed that was exactly what they were getting!

"Get ready for another sprint! Forget the mud! Forget the weather! SOLDIERS, DO YOU HEAR ME?!" Edge wasn't even waiting for Sid's instructions now—but then he, too, burst out laughing.

The scene in front of him was just too funny: Swift was trying to rub the mud off her jersey, but she'd smeared it into a big circle, giving herself a

teddy bear tummy; Bond's forehead mud had worked its way into her hair; Mouth's pants and socks were covered in grass stains and mud; and Lucas, who was dirty up to his elbows, had so many pieces of grass stuck to the side of his face that it looked like he needed a shave!

Lucas had never laughed so hard. Bond had the biggest smile he'd ever seen. And even through the mud on their faces, Swift and Mouth Guard were beaming.

Their trainer, on the other hand, had barely broken a sweat—and he was perfectly clean!

Sid was laughing, too, but he wanted to get the Chips to the top of the hill, where he said there'd be even more areas for them to train.

"Great!" Bond said sarcastically, working hard to keep up with her taller teammates.

They were exhausted, but none of them seemed able to resist Sid's calm, friendly voice: "Now ten jumping jacks, one front roll—and we'll run all the way to the top!"

"AND GET THOSE KNEES UP!" Edge yelled, grinning, as they all took off.

CHAPTER 11

"*Wow*—this is *awesome!*"

Lucas, who was now massaging the cramp under his rib cage, couldn't believe what the Chips were seeing. None of them could.

At the top of the hill, the grass merged with a gigantic stone wall, or rampart. There was a long, deep indent behind it—almost a ditch or a waterless moat— and then a second wall with grass on top, making it look like a fortress growing out of the earth.

Edge, who loved anything military, was amazed.

"And this *view*! It's so *big*!" Swift said, turning around in a circle to see how far they'd come. From the top of the hill, they could see the water stretched out in front of them. Through the haze, they could still make out the small island they'd passed in the trawler, the many buildings that made up the harbour, and what

Sid said was the Macdonald Bridge—a huge metal structure that reached all the way to another city.

If the storm hits the harbour again—if there's more of it, Swift thought excitedly, *there's no way we'll miss it from here.*

While a few of the Ice Chips checked out the long black cannons that were peeking out over the wall, Lucas took a moment to get closer to Edge. He knew what Bond was going to ask them: *How do we get home?* And he had no idea what to tell her . . .

In fact, the moment he'd considered the question, Lucas had shuddered. How *were* they going to get home from here?

When they'd last leaped through time, Edge, Swift, and Lucas had skated against the wind on an outdoor rink in Saskatchewan, and then—*poof!*—they'd found themselves back skating on their own ice in Riverton. But there was no rink here—or not one they'd be allowed to use. So how were they supposed to leave the harbour? *By swimming?!*

"I've seen this view before," Edge said in an exaggerated voice as Lucas got closer. "And the clock tower."

"Great—*anything* that can help us. If we can figure out how to—" Lucas started to say, but Edge cut him off.

"It's in this video my mom loves. The Maritime Bhangra Group—you know those guys? The Sikhs who make viral dance videos where they're shovelling snow or dancing near the beach? They filmed one here—right here!"

Why is he talking about videos when we could be stuck here with no way home? Lucas wondered, taken aback.

That's when Swift approached them, her cheeks still rosy after the big run, and whispered out of the side of her mouth: "Shhh! Lucas, we can't talk now."

"You came for training, remember?" Edge was now whispering, too, trying to look like he wasn't talking at all. "This guy is good—*really good*. Learn from him first . . . then we'll worry about everything else."

"What *is* this place?" Bond asked Sid, marvelling at how the entire structure seemed to be built in the shape of a star—all long walls and pointy corners.

"A pirate hideout?" guessed Mouth Guard. "A secret spy camp? An *alien* base?"

Sid was grinning as he walked the Chips over to an opening in the wall, where a soldier in a red jacket, a fluffy black hat, and a Scottish kilt was standing stone-faced and ignoring them.

"*This* is the Citadel," Sid said proudly as he led the kids through a stone archway, over a bridge that crossed the ditch, and into a wide, funny-shaped courtyard.

"This must be a tough day to be a guard," Edge said, impressed. "You have to keep a straight face no matter what—can't even complain about the horrible weather!"

"Okay, but what's a citadel *for*?" Mouth Guard asked, looking at the three-storey stone buildings that now stood in front of them.

"It's a fort that was built to protect the city—built by the British more than two hundred years ago. It's been rebuilt four times, and this last one was finished in 1856," Sid said, smiling like a tour guide. "In Halifax, this is almost sacred ground." With a mischievous grin, he added: "It's also one of our best training facilities."

"You train *inside* the Citadel, too?" Lucas asked between quiet gulps of air. He was still puffing from the hill but trying to hide it.

"Sure," Sid said with a friendly smirk, motioning toward the many stone staircases along the walls of the courtyard.

"So—who likes *stairs*?!"

✵ ✵ ✵

The Ice Chips were doubled over, puffing and coughing, by the time they saw the soldier from the gate leading a small group of wet visitors across the courtyard. He was waving his arm, telling the tour group to follow him toward a building without even saying a word.

A half hour earlier, Sid had bet the Chips that they wouldn't be able to run all of the stairs with him—up one set and down another until they'd made their way around the entire courtyard.

Lucas had done his best, but he'd found it a tough grind. He was hardly alone. Sid had raced up and down the uneven steps like he was flying—dancing sideways on the way up, sometimes taking two steps at a time, and then jumping down again, three at a time.

Edge was shocked that none of the park employees they'd passed—all dressed in period costumes—had burst out laughing as the group of dirty, heavy-breathing kids ran by. Of course, with the rain and the wind, they were probably all busy trying to keep warm!

That wasn't a problem for the Ice Chips. By the end of their circuit, they were pouring with sweat. Their legs stung. Their butts hurt. Their feet were sore from jumping. Their brains were still spinning from making sure every step and jump landed perfectly on the hundreds of uneven steps.

Finally, Sid had stopped running and sagged, catching his breath. The Ice Chips caught up and did the same. All anyone could hear was the loud gasping for breath; all six kids had their hands on their knees and were sucking air back into their lungs as if they'd spent the last ten minutes under water.

Then Sid saw the soldier with the tour group and had another idea . . .

With the mud slowly drying on their equipment, the Chips watched as he ran over to his parents for a moment and then quietly tucked himself into the back of the visitors' group, signalling for the other kids to join him.

"Is this part of the training?" Swift asked once she stood shoulder to shoulder with Sid, her lungs still burning. "Do they put you in jail and you have to dig your way out?"

"You'd be surprised," Sid whispered. "This is a little different . . . but it will definitely get your hearts racing!"

The door of the building had just opened and a man

dressed in black with a swinging lantern was now calling them all inside.

"I must warn you," the shadowy guide whispered as he led the tour group into a small, dark room, "this is a ghost tour, but the stories you are about to hear actually happened . . . here, in this citadel. Ask any of our employees—especially the ones who work the night shifts." He had a deadly serious look on his face, but Lucas could tell the guide was enjoying this. "Oh, and if you hear the windows rattling a little more than usual today, it *could* be the hurricane, or it could be . . . well, something else . . . "

Lucas shivered. Edge felt chills. And Bond decided she wasn't letting Sid out of her sight.

"Follow me," the man with the lantern said as he turned and walked deeper into the darkness. "Careful not to fall too far behind."

The tour group walked up and down many stairs, through narrow doorways and dark halls, listening to tales of how the fort was built, how it had never actually come under attack, and how it was *haunted*.

"One of our resident ghosts is the Grey Lady," the guide said. "We used to have a worker who sat in a chair right over there, and one day, this woman in a flowing

white dress came in, sobbing. When the worker stood up to greet her, she just vanished"—the guide snapped his fingers loudly—"and after that . . . well, every time he sat in that same chair, he swore he could smell her perfume."

Lucas's heartbeat quickened and his palms started to sweat.

"Sometimes workers think they hear the Grey Lady moving in the halls above them," the guide continued, swinging his lantern around the dark room, "or walking, very slowly, up and down the steps of one of our hidden staircases."

Sid was giggling. He'd probably heard these stories a dozen times. "Come on," he whispered to the five Ice Chips as the tour moved down another hallway. "Let's get some more training in."

"There's *more*?!" Lucas asked, his heart still pounding.

CHAPTER 12

There was definitely more. Lots more.

"Sid's amazing!"

"He is!"

The kids had just spilled back out into the mist-filled courtyard, and already Sid had them moving again.

"He's like a machine!" Lucas said under his breath as he fell in with the group. First was a lunge with the right leg, then a lunge with the left, and then ten very slow squats.

"You're killing us!" said Swift, laughing.

He must know the coaches will pick him—or put him on their lists, thought Lucas. *That's how Sid can keep going, keep training so hard.*

He probably doesn't even bite his nails.

"Who can go the lowest?" Sid asked with a friendly smirk before looking around for their next challenge.

"He'd better not be looking at those stairs," Bond moaned as she went too low and tipped over onto the wet ground.

"You know," Sid's mom said, grinning as she approached the little exercise group, "maybe you should try on some of the dress-up clothes they have here. The soldier ones. Warm up a bit."

"Yeah, get into something dry for a few minutes!" Sid's dad chuckled as Taylor bounced along in his arms, smiling at Swift.

But Sid had already taken off running, with Mouth Guard following close behind.

When Sid returned a moment later, his arms were piled high with red, white, and black material.

"*Un-be-lievable!*" Edge shouted excitedly.

Sid's arms were loaded up with enough uniforms to dress an entire army (or a hockey team!): shirts, kilts, red Highland coats, socks, boots, and little bonnets bearing a brass badge for the 78th Highlanders.

"Thank you!" Bond and Swift yelled, each pulling on a coat and a pair of socks. The wind was starting to pick up again—and they needed to stay warm!

"Sure," said Sid. "You can even shoot rifles over there, and play drums, but—"

"Umm, anyone know how to *juggle*?"

Mouth Guard was back, and his arms were full, too—with a very odd assortment of items. He had juggling pins, a heavy-looking sandbag, a long rope, a bag of chalk, and a small ladder with only five rungs.

"Whaaat?" Mouth Guard said, smiling. "The guard there said I could borrow whatever I wanted."

Bond rolled her eyes. "So you took *everything*?"

"No, no, this'll be great," Sid said as he wriggled himself into a kilt and slipped his arms into a bright red coat. "Playing baseball has helped me a lot with hockey. You don't always need a stick and a puck to train."

"Fun!" said Swift, excited for their next competition.

"I'm in!" Edge cheered as he tossed Lucas a red coat with gold buttons.

* * *

"I don't want to play a *little* kid's game!" Mouth Guard whined. With an oversized coat and his hat on crooked, he did look a bit like a toddler, but no one was going to point that out.

"You're the one who found the chalk," Swift said matter-of-factly. "You don't want to get any better?"

"No-n-n-no," Mouth Guard stuttered. "Well, yeah, but ... "

"We're *all* going to do it," said Edge, delighted by their new training plan.

Sid was on the ground, busy with the huge piece of chalk. He'd found a long platform-like area where the cannons were rolled out, and on the smooth stone surface, he was drawing what had to be the world's largest game of ... *hopscotch*.

"Who wants a turn?" he asked as he finished his twenty-seventh hopscotch box. The boxes led off in all directions, but that's how Sid had intended it. Excited, he moved back to the beginning. From there, they'd leap, hop, and dance their way through the game—like soldiers running through a mess of tires.

Swift was right behind Sid for the first run, followed by Edge, Lucas, Bond, and Mouth Guard.

Somehow, as he had on the stairs, Sid seemed to know exactly what he was doing. He flew across the board, hitting each box separately: first the left foot touching down, then the right foot crossing over to land in the next box, then back in the other direction.

The Ice Chips weren't quite so graceful. Swift did okay (she often practised this kind of thing in track), but Edge got confused and leaped the wrong way, crashing into Lucas (and Lucas's elbow) in mid-flight. They collided with a smack, and a moment later, they were both on the ground in a heap. But at least they were laughing.

The next challenge belonged to Lucas, but he kind of regretted it once they got started.

Sid was the first to hold the ladder upright, as Lucas had suggested, grasping the top of it because it wasn't leaning on anything. Then, using balance and strength, he climbed almost to the top rung and back down, with the ladder hardly even moving.

The others followed and did okay, but Lucas got only as high as the second rung—it was harder than he'd thought!

"You don't like losing." Sid smiled sympathetically in Lucas's direction. "Neither do I, but that's why we keep practising!"

Luckily, Edge was already in position for the next game: the sandbag.

CHAPTER 13

Edge's heart was beating wildly.

Bond had tied one end of the rope around the sand-bag and the other around Edge's waist. The idea was to have the Chips drag the bag behind them to build up their strength.

"From here to the wall, okay?" Swift said, getting ready to time her friend with her comm-band.

Edge had to work hard, but he did fine. Then Sid did well, as usual. Mouth Guard put some of his extra energy into it and was surprisingly fast. Lucas was in the middle of the pack—but he felt good. Then it was Bond's turn.

Bond was bent so far forward, she looked as if her nose would scrape the ground. The strain was incred-ible. She was sweating hard. Every few seconds, she stopped, caught her breath, grunted, and then again pushed as hard as she could with her feet.

"Go, Bond!" Swift shouted, looking at her watch. Bond was slow, but she was doing it!

"It's ... so ... *heavy!*" she squealed between gasps for air.

If she could do *this*, Bond thought, then she'd definitely force herself to tell the Chips her secret when they got home. Talking would be hard, but she knew she *had* to get rid of that other horrible heavy weight she'd been dragging around.

"Remember—you're *smaller* than the other players on the ice," Sid called after her, still a little out of breath from his own iron man pull. "If you use that, and really crouch down in the corners, they'll never get the puck away from you."

Bond tried to get even lower, ignoring the burning pain in her legs.

When she finally collapsed against the wall, she was smiling.

"What's up next?" Sid asked excitedly, scooping up one of the juggling pins and tossing it to Mouth Guard.

"You juggle, too?" Lucas asked. *Is there no end to this kid's skills?*

"Only with my stick and a puck," Sid said, tossing Mouth Guard the other two pins.

Mouth Guard now had all three pins in his hands,

but all he did was toss the blue one up a few times and then catch it again.

"You guys know Paul Kariya?" Sid asked.

"Of course," Swift said. "He's in the Hall of Fame—but he quit hockey to become a surfer!"

"Actually, he didn't," corrected Lucas, who'd learned a lot about different players as he copied pictures of them into his journal. "He's in the Hall of Fame, yeah, but he quit hockey because of too many hits to the head—too many concussions. Kariya said he *had* to retire."

Sid looked at them oddly.

"What do you mean? Kariya's not retired," Sid corrected the corrector. "He only started with the Anaheim Ducks *last year*!"

"Kariya . . . he's just starting out?" Mouth Guard asked, confused, but Bond hip checked him from the side, forcing him to close his mouth.

The year! thought Lucas, wishing that he could pull out his journal without being caught by Sid. *If Kariya just started playing with the Ducks last year—that means we're in . . . 1996?*

"Anyway, Kariya says juggling's great for hand–eye coordination," said Sid, not noticing the bizarre looks the Chips were shooting each other. "And that's what makes a top scorer, right?"

"I can score, I just can't pass," Mouth Guard said without any insecurity. He tossed up a red pin and then a blue one, but they just crossed and fell to the ground. There was no way he'd ever get all three dancing in the air.

"Can I try?" asked Swift. Before she'd started hockey and track, she said, her parents had put her and her sister through rhythmic gymnastics.

Sid and the Chips watched as Swift tossed one of the pins into the air, quickly followed by a second, then a third. They would fly up, spin, and come down, and in a flash, she would catch them perfectly and send them flying again.

Magic, Lucas thought. *Pure magic.*

"You have to *throw* the pin into the right spot — that's the trick. Don't worry about *catching* it," Swift said as her eyes moved back and forth, watching the pins. "If you've thrown it right, the pin will be there when you grab for it."

"Just like a pass in hockey," added Sid. "You're supposed to think about where that puck *needs* to be. You shoot ahead of your guy — into the *future* — and if you've done it right, the player will be there to grab it."

At the word "future" Lucas shuddered, but Sid didn't seem to notice.

"You mean I don't shoot to a person?" asked Mouth Guard. "I shoot to a *place*?"

"YES!" the other Ice Chips all yelled at once.

* * *

The Ice Chips had just returned everything they'd borrowed from the Citadel—the clothes and coats, the ladder and sandbag—when a light rain began to fall. The guard who accepted the clothes said he'd seen flashes in the distance—lightning—but the kids didn't think they'd heard any thunder yet.

"It looks like the storm really is going to hit us again—maybe it never really left," Swift said as she pulled a stray strand of hair from her face. She was looking up at the darkening sky, and Lucas could tell she wished she could see more of the water, to watch the storm roll in. "This is going to be a big one."

"This isn't Halifax's first hurricane, but it's best to be careful," Sid's mom agreed.

"Just one more run?" Sid pleaded, tightening the strings on his hood. "It'll be fast, I promise."

"Aw, come on—really?" Mouth Guard said, groaning.

"I'll die!" said Swift.

Sid laughed. "No, you guys can do this."

And off he headed, with the five Ice Chips in tow, bolting toward a far corner of the fort. There was an opening there, but it was almost too dark to see anything at the bottom of it.

Still smiling, Sid led them into the darkness.

He danced down the uneven stone steps and the Chips did the same, all the way to the bottom.

It was dark. It was damp. It was dank, Lucas thought—a word his bompa sometimes used to describe an old abandoned garage at the end of the gravel road near the cottage.

"Okay, so here I race to the top as fast as I can, then I come down skipping two steps at a time, then up again backwards and back down skipping three— and I keep going until I'm about to fall over," Sid said. "Who's with me?"

The Ice Chips slowly raised their hands.

"Okay, go!" Sid shouted and took off, fast.

Up the uneven stone steps the Chips and their new trainer flew. They reached the top and leaped down two at a time, then raced up again, then back down. Again and again.

Lucas's lungs were burning. He knew he could make it to the bottom once more, but that was it.

The others clearly felt the same. When Lucas made it down again, Swift was there at the base of the dark staircase, crouched over and gasping. Edge's face was as red as a stoplight, and Bond was holding her sides. Mouth Guard, thankfully, was silent, swallowing air like it was life-giving water.

Lucas looked around, but with the storm rolling in overhead and no light on, he couldn't make out much of what was in the shadows surrounding them.

Then they heard a clink. The sound of a door opening. A door creaking. Footsteps, like old leather shoes on a hidden staircase.

And then a moan.

"*AAAAAAAOOOOOOOOOHHHHHHHH-HAAAAAAAAAAAYYYYY!*"

The Grey Lady!

Instantly, Lucas's lungs filled with fresh oxygen. His legs found new muscles. His boots moved like they were tied to rocket blasters.

The Chips flew up the stone steps so fast that Lucas wondered if they'd ever be able to stop.

Up, up, up they ran, into the rain and wind that was

now swirling through the courtyard. When they were far enough away, they collapsed, their hearts pounding in their ears.

But where are Sid and Mouth Guard?

They weren't with them. And Lucas hadn't seen them running up the steps . . .

He quickly sat up and looked toward the staircase. Nothing.

He waited. Still nothing.

Could they still be down . . . *there*?

Just then, the kids saw something moving above the opening to the staircase—something round.

It was bobbing, rising slowly . . . and it had a big *C* on it—for the Montreal Canadiens! It was Sid's baseball cap, on top of Sid's head. He was walking up the stairs toward them!

And he was smiling—and moaning . . .

"AAAAAAAOOOOOOOOOHHHHHHHH-HAAAAAAAAAAYYYYY!"

Lucas's heart had skipped a beat. Edge looked angry, and Bond just rolled her eyes.

And then another loud, rolling sound floated up from the bottom of the staircase . . .

PPPPFFFFWWWWHHHHHHHEEEEEEEEEEE-EEEEET!!!!!

CHAPTER 14

"MOUTH GUARD!" the Chips all yelled at once, their voices rising and falling like trombones. Their fart-throwing teammate was now bounding up the stairs behind Sid, laughing his head off.

"That Grey Lady has some *serious* gas!" Mouth Guard snorted.

"That's so rude!" shouted Swift, trying to keep in a giggle.

"And mean!" added Edge. He was laughing so hard he was crying.

Lucas was about to say something, too, but he was interrupted — by the sudden blast of an explosion!

As fast as they could, the Chips all moved to cover their ears. But that single blast was the only one.

Then the smell of gunpowder came floating through the air.

And the sound of . . . *bagpipes*?

"Ahhh!" Sid yelled. "The Citadel fires its cannon at noon! I'M LATE FOR THE SKATE!"

Sid's parents had already put Taylor into her car seat, but they didn't know what to do with the other kids' stuff.

"It's okay—go!" said Lucas, not wanting to slow Sid down. "We're going to find someone at the Five Fishermen restaurant. We'll run down the hill and meet you at the bottom!"

"*If* you don't mind bringing our sticks and things down for us," Swift added, winking at Taylor through the window.

"We'll be fast," Edge said with a proud smile. "We've been training."

The Five Fishermen, they'd seen on their way up, was across the street from the big arena where Sid was about to skate. While Edge had docked the boat, Captain Brannen had told him that he ate lunch there every day. Swift had decided that was their only option: find Brannen, and then find their way back to Riverton. Last time, they'd landed near a rink and had leaped back home after skating as hard as they could. This time, Brannen's boat seemed like their best choice.

Sid jumped into the back seat beside Taylor just as Lucas and his teammates took off running.

Tired but determined, the Chips sped down the hill as the rain started to fall harder and harder. Halfway down, Lucas slipped on the mud and fell on his butt. Leaning in over his shoulder, Bond reached out her arm to help him up.

"I guess *now* isn't a good time to explain?" she said over the howling wind.

"We aren't sure how to get home from here, if that's what you're asking," Lucas said, wiping a splash of mud from his cheek. "Now you know as much as we do."

* * *

"Are you ready for your rematch tomorrow?" Sid asked with a smile. "Mouth Guard said something about it." He was rushing, but he still wanted to say goodbye.

The five Chips were beside him, standing under an awning in front of the blue-glass entrance of the big arena, taking their things out of the van as fast as they could.

"Sid, let's get moving," his dad said. "I know you

like to step onto the ice last, but you don't want to be *too* late."

"Yeah, I know," Sid said, hoisting his hockey bag onto his shoulder. "Just one more thing."

Lucas was about to put his helmet back on, to protect his head from the rain that was now falling in big, heavy drops just beyond the awning, when Sid stepped up to him and punched him in the arm.

"You know," Sid said, "if you're in better shape than the other players, it'll show in your game. And you're good, I can see it. Keep training."

All Lucas felt at that moment was exhausted—and wet—but he hoped what Sid was saying was true . . . or could be true.

Then Sid shot Bond a big smile. "And you—even if you don't have the other players' natural skills, you can always make something happen on the ice if you work hard enough. That's what I try to do."

As Sid waved to the others and moved toward the doors, Bond just looked down at the sidewalk. She was embarrassed and didn't want to tell the other Ice Chips why. Only Mouth Guard knew her secret. But soon, the rest of her teammates would, too.

Mouth Guard started gushing the moment their

new friend was out of sight. "Sid's awesome! What a coach! He even let us shoot on his basement net when we were at his house . . . "

The Chips were now hurrying down Carmichael Street in the rain, on their way to the Five Fishermen.

"Well, I guess *I* shot on the net, but Bond shot on Sid's parents' *laundry machine*," Mouth Guard said.

"I didn't *try* to shoot the dryer!" Bond yelled, gently jabbing her elbow into Mouth Guard's ribs. "Sid had taught me how to flick my wrist, and then the puck just flew!"

"She even left a big black mark on it!" Mouth Guard laughed, giving Lucas an image of an old beat-up dryer full of little black dents—an image that somehow felt familiar . . .

When the Ice Chips finally reached the stone-and-clapboard restaurant, they noticed that the storm was again wreaking havoc in the city. The trees in the park across Argyle Street were now swaying back and forth like dandelions—some were almost bent in half! The gutters along the sidewalk had become streams, and cars were plowing into puddles as their drivers tried to push their way through.

"Is that . . . *part of a roof*?" Bond asked, pointing to

a chunk of dark shingles that had just blown into the park. She was holding on to her helmet as though the wind might blow it off. Underneath it, her braids were flying around like windsocks.

"We have to get more bottled water and bread— more supplies!" a man yelled to a woman as the two of them—one with giant boots and the other with an inside-out umbrella—went splashing past.

"We told Sid's parents we'd take cover in the restaurant until this was over," said Swift, feeling guilty that they'd somehow brought Bond and Mouth Guard into this storm with them. "We'd better get in there—*fast*!"

But they *couldn't* get into the restaurant—no one could. A sign outside the tall historic building said it didn't open until 4 p.m.!

"They're not even *open* at lunchtime?! But Captain Brannen—" Edge started to say, confused.

Lucas was tucking himself into the arch of the doorway, unzipping his backpack, and hurriedly fishing out his journal.

The wind was turning the pages for him as he searched—the pages that had finally dried out—and soon Lucas had what he was looking for: a drawing of a beat-up clothes dryer.

This dryer, however, had more than just one tiny scratch. It looked as though it had withstood an artillery barrage in a nasty war. It had been dented and dinged, as if someone had dropped it from the top of the CN Tower. Lucas's dryer was bashed in, warped, and covered in black streaks . . . and it was legendary.

It had once lived in the basement of the most gifted NHL scorer Lucas had ever seen touch steel to ice— the player he'd drawn, with a big friendly smile, on the very next page.

Both the dryer and the smile belong to *Sidney Crosby*.

CHAPTER 15

"I guess we don't have to worry about Sid being late for his big break!" Bond said. She'd just started playing hockey, but even she knew that Sidney Crosby had grown up to become one of the game's greatest scorers.

All day in the rain, they'd been training with the future captain of the Pittsburgh Penguins and of Canada's gold medal Olympic team—and they hadn't had a clue! Their new friend would soon be known around the hockey world as Sid the Kid—number 87. The Next One. The great Captain Canada!

Edge's eyes were wide. Mouth Guard's mouth was hanging open. And Swift's cheeks were flushed with embarrassment. "Oh, wow!" she exclaimed. "And you know that *Taylor* Crosby—that little baby!—grows up to be an awesome goalie, right?"

Lucas laughed, but only because he was almost crying. Sidney—Sid, the guy who'd saved his life—had gone on to win almost every hockey trophy imaginable: the Art Ross Trophy, the Hart Memorial Trophy, the Stanley Cup (again and again!), and Olympic gold medals.

"No wonder he was so good at everything!" Lucas said as he stuffed his journal back into his bag.

"Unbelievable!" Edge muttered to himself as a gust of wind blew up against the restaurant, almost knocking the Ice Chips over.

Someone, somewhere had door chimes that were clashing wildly in the wind. And a nearby tree, bent as far as it could, tipped over with a loud ripping noise and slammed down onto the road beside them.

"We've gotta get out of here!" Swift cried.

"There's only one place I can think to go," Edge said warily, pointing down the dark street ahead of them . . .

The one that led down to the harbour.

❄ ❄ ❄

"Look for Brannen's trawler!" Edge called to the group once they were near the pier.

"*Even* if he's not on it," added Swift. "Maybe all we need is to get into the storage room on his boat. We won't know until we get there."

Swift went left with Lucas and Bond. Edge went right with Mouth Guard.

The two groups moved as quickly as they could, scanning the boats in the harbour.

"Brannen's not here," Swift said, disappointed. Lucas agreed. It was as though the captain and his boat had just disappeared. "You don't think his trawler *sank* after we—"

"Guys, come *here*!" Edge called excitedly in their direction. He was out of breath. And he'd found something.

"The *boat*!" Lucas cheered under his breath as Swift and Bond turned around and started running.

But it wasn't the boat—at least, not Brannen's.

Mouth Guard and Edge had found two fishermen in long, thick raincoats—one blue and one green—struggling to tie up a small old rowboat with peeling yellow paint.

"They found it abandoned, floating out in the storm," Mouth Guard said quietly as they approached the two friendly looking fishermen.

"Like we said, it's not ours. You can use it if you're

really that desperate to get out on the water," said the fisherman in green.

Are we desperate? Lucas wondered nervously. *Should* anyone *be out in this weather?*

"But we wouldn't recommend it," added the man in blue. "That storm's a mean one."

"Wait! You think we should take a boat out to go find Brannen?" Swift asked Edge, confused.

"Not exactly," he said, taking another step toward the fishermen. "Can you repeat what you said about the Five Fishermen, if you don't mind?"

"What, that it's *haunted*?" the man in blue asked, grinning. He pulled his rope through its final loop, then grabbed another line. "That's what yer out in this weather for? A ghost story?"

"Got good seafood," the man in green chimed in. "But there's nothin' at noon—like you asked about. The only ones who eat lunch at the Five Fishermen are the ghosts!"

The man in green started moaning playfully, just as Sid had, while his friend shook with laughter.

"Ghosts?" Bond mouthed, looking at Lucas, then Edge. "Again?!"

"Yeah. Well, it's part 'a history, isn't it?" said the

guy in green, once he'd finished with both his moaning and his knots. "The Five Fishermen used to be a funeral home. There's supposed to be ghosts there from 1917 — from the Halifax Explosion — and even some from the *Titanic*, the famous boat that sank in 1912."

"The people who survived the sinking of the *Titanic* were taken to New York," said the man in blue. "But the ones who didn't . . . they were brought here to Halifax."

When the fishermen finally started walking back to their own boat, still chuckling about their stories, Edge spun around to face his teammates.

"There's no lunch at the Five Fishermen — there's no Brannen. They said they'd never met him." His eyes were wide. He was completely freaked out. "The captain's gotta be a ghost. That's why we can't find him!"

"Are you *serious*? You believed them?" Bond asked, surprised.

"Even if the captain *is* a ghost, this storm is *real*," said Lucas, glancing nervously at the rising water.

"*Is* the storm real?" asked Mouth Guard. He'd been staring at the beat-up boat and ignoring the ghost talk all together. "Or do you think we *made* it happen? I mean, could our leap have *caused* it somehow?"

Bond scoffed at the idea, but Swift was following

his train of thought. "You think the storm might be *part* of our leap—like, it could be . . . our portal?"

Lucas's mind was racing. For the past ten minutes, he'd been watching a wide, dark cloud inch its way across the water, almost like a moving blanket. And now it had sparks of lightning flaring inside it. The hurricane was rolling through, and he couldn't help feeling that it was coming back to meet them.

"Portal? Wait—you mean you *do* want to go out in that rowboat?" Bond was shocked. She couldn't believe what she was hearing. "You're not supposed to be on *water* in a lightning storm. You know that, right?"

"We've got to try *something*," Edge said as he tossed his bag and hockey stick into the boat. He climbed in, and Swift and Mouth Guard followed. "Hand me the compass," he called to Lucas. "And pull out your brother's night light—we're going to need it."

"Are you going, too?" Bond asked Lucas, horrified. "But what if they're wrong?"

"It's scary, I know," said Swift, pulling a life jacket out from under her seat.

There was a flash of lightning, then a loud boom, causing all of them to jump.

"Just look on the side of the boat, guys," Mouth

Guard said, speaking more slowly and carefully than any of his teammates had ever heard him. "We'll be fine."

Bond and Lucas both leaned sideways. Through the falling rain and peeling paint, they could barely make out the name, scratched into the side of the rowboat. But it was there, just where the others had seen it before they'd climbed in.

The Ice Chip.

"You're the superstitious one," Edge said, looking at Lucas with a gentle smirk. "Gotta be a sign from the hockey gods, don't you think?"

CHAPTER 16
Riverton

Out in the swirling grey of the storm, surrounded by white-capped waves, the Ice Chips paddled.

They were getting closer to the thick, whirling winds when a flash suddenly lit up the dark sky.

There was a cracking, splitting sound . . .

Like the earth being forced open.

And then . . .

BOOM!

The five Ice Chips were tumbling across the red line on their home ice, as though they'd just been tipped out of a boat.

Lucas was gasping for air, afraid he'd be pulled under water again. Edge was lying on his stomach, still looking down at the compass in his hands, its needle now spinning and spinning. Bond was on her knees, blinking in the bright arena lights. And Swift had tripped and fallen over Mouth Guard's legs . . .

Wait—is Mouth Guard swimming?

Lucas didn't mean to, but he started to giggle.

When Mouth Guard realized that he hadn't actually fallen into the water, but instead was lying on the ice back home in Riverton, he stopped moving. A drawn-out "ooooh" escaped his lips, and everyone burst out laughing.

Even Crunch, who was sitting in the stands filming everything with his tablet, thought it was funny.

When the Chips had suddenly reappeared, Crunch was still finishing the sentence he'd started yelling at the time that they'd made their leap: " . . . record *everything*!"

The leaping Chips had heard the first part—the "Don't forget to"—hours earlier: before the storm, before Sid, before the Citadel. But for Crunch, it had all come out in the same breath. For him, no time had passed at all.

"Ugh, ow!" Edge yelled as he slipped on the water that was dripping off their equipment.

"Are we . . . *home*?" This felt like their rink and smelled like their rink, but Mouth Guard could barely believe it.

"Let me see the video!" Crunch was already running onto the ice in his boots, slipping excitedly and reaching for the backpack beside Lucas.

"You don't want to know if we're okay?" Lucas asked, laughing as he handed over the pack. He'd been scared out on the water, pushing through those ferocious waves, but now that they were back where they'd started, it seemed as if it could all have been a dream.

"You don't want to know what *happened to us*?" Bond asked in shock. *We're soaking wet, we've been gone for hours, and all Crunch cares about is his silly camera?*

"Yes—uh, of course. But first . . . *where* in the world did you end up?" Crunch sputtered, eagerly opening the pack and checking the camera. "And more importantly . . . *who* did you meet?!"

✳ ✳ ✳

"No, I mean the *player*—not the puck!" Mouth Guard said, getting excited. "Sid told me that I should picture the *player*—the one I'm passing to—as a moving train."

"So he can try to predict where the player is going," Swift explained. "And make sure that's where the puck lands."

"Good advice," Crunch said. He was impressed that they'd met Crosby, but he was only half paying attention. He was busy pushing buttons on his camera, trying to get the video sent to his tablet.

"And guess what? I lifted a puck off the ground!" Bond said, beaming. "Sid said most kids get the puck too far out in front of them—but you need leverage. He showed me how to shoot from the back foot and then use the flex in my stick to lift it."

"Bond even hit Sid's dryer!" said Lucas. He was giggling, but he was also slightly jealous.

"I saw that dryer once. In a museum. I'll just . . . oh, here we go." Crunch took the tablet from Edge and tapped a few buttons on the screen.

Edge had been reading online about Halifax Harbour. Apparently, there *had* been a Captain Horatio Brannen—only he'd died in the Halifax Explosion . . . on December 6, 1917.

"Creepy!" Swift said when Edge told them what he'd confirmed: many people who'd died in the explosion *really were* taken to what is now the Five Fishermen restaurant.

Bond gasped and looked at Lucas. A moment later, the video was playing.

First, they saw white—the boards around their rink. Then their ice surface, which was bobbing along because Lucas was moving. Next they could hear Lucas, Swift, and Edge skating, and see Mouth Guard and Bond stepping onto the ice behind them . . .

There was a bright flash—was it lightning? Then a loud buzzing as the screen switched to fuzz—pixels flitting across it like miniature snowflakes. The only sound was "*Shhhhhhhh-zzzzzzzzzzz!*"

"It didn't work?!" Crunch yelled in frustration, shaking his tablet as though that could bring the image back. "Wait—could the electromagnetic field somehow have interfered with the—"

"It did work, kind of," interrupted Mouth Guard. He was pointing at the video control bar at the bottom of the screen. "You've only got static—but you've got *six hours* of it."

"That proves we were *somewhere*," Lucas said positively.

"It's gone, but at least we'll remember our training," Swift said, trying to sound upbeat. "That will really help our game this year."

"Yeah, this year . . . " Bond mumbled as she very quietly began to cry.

Most of the kids were still watching the tablet, but Mouth Guard had seen her face change—and he knew why.

"Wait!" he boomed. "You still haven't told them you quit?"

CHAPTER 17

"You what?!" Edge couldn't believe it.

"How could you do that?" cried Swift.

"Why didn't you tell us?" asked Lucas, completely shocked.

"That's what we were coming to say when we stepped out onto the ice after you guys. Mouth was with me for moral support," Bond explained apologetically. "I just . . . wanted to skate with my teammates one last time."

"She thought she was dragging down the team—we both were," Mouth Guard said sympathetically. "So she asked her dad to talk to Coach Small at the parents' dinner and tell him she was done with hockey for good."

Lucas shook his head. He'd never heard anything so bananas. *Done with hockey? For good?*

"But now I *don't* want to quit," said Bond with tears in her eyes. "Not after training with Sid!"

"Then don't," said Edge matter-of-factly.

"But what if my dad's already talked to Coach Small? I'm probably too late!" Bond sobbed.

"You might be," Crunch agreed, checking the time on his comm-band. "The party's already started."

"It's started, but it's not over yet," said Swift, suddenly determined.

"We'd better hurry!" Lucas shouted as he grabbed Bond by the arm.

* * *

"Where are we going? Where *is* the mayor's house?" Bond yelled as the six Ice Chips burst through the front doors of the arena and took off running along the river.

"Top of the hill over there," Crunch said, pointing into the distance. He was breathing heavily and working hard to keep up with his teammates. Was it possible that they were in better shape already?

"Are you sure we should crash the party?" Mouth Guard asked. He was nervous. Sneaking into the rink was one thing, but sneaking into the mayor's house was a whole new level.

"Of course we should!" shouted Swift, jumping

over the curb and then a small shrub as if she were running hurdles.

"It's our mission, guys—we have to keep Bond
on this team," Lucas said as he pumped his legs even
harder. Soon they turned a corner at Celian Street and
were all racing up Riverton's biggest hill.

❖ ❖ ❖

Standing in front of the heavy red door of the mayor's
house, Bond lifted her hand, curled it into a fist, and
banged hard three times.

Nothing.

"Let *me* see!" Mouth Guard begged as he pushed
her out of the way and crouched so he could look
through the mail slot. He could see bodies moving—
someone's hand with a wedding ring walking by, and
two people's bellies laughing.

"I still can't see anything!" he said. "Knock again.
Really bang!"

"Why does the party have to be so *loud*?!" com-
plained Swift. Climbing the hill to the mayor's house
had been brutal, but getting someone to answer
the door was mission impossible. They'd rung the

doorbell, yelled, stomped, and knocked, but it didn't seem that anyone could hear them at all.

"It's too bad the mayor doesn't have a dog," said Mouth Guard, letting Bond back in front of the mail slot again. "If there were a dog door, one of us could probably squeeze through it and get inside."

"If the mayor had a dog, Mouth Guard, it would probably chase us and bite our butts," said Swift, rolling her eyes.

The Chips had heard music playing and parents laughing, even before they'd seen the house. There were tons of cars parked along the curb; the party was packed. Once they'd figured out that no one could hear the doorbell, the Chips split up just as they had in the harbour: Edge had gone around the left to tap on windows, Crunch had gone to the right, and Lucas was trying the back door. But so far, they were all being ignored.

Through the mail slot, Bond could now see Coach Small walking by with a breaded shrimp and a glass of punch in his hand . . . and her father, looking as deflated as a flat tire. Mr. Foster was right behind the coach, about to tap him on the shoulder!

"He's going to tell Coach Small! We've got to get

in there! They'll replace me!" Bond yelled, but still no one inside could hear her.

"We need a loud noise! Something louder than our voices—louder than knocking!" Swift declared.

"What if we all yell together?" asked Lucas, who was bounding back up the steps with the others.

"Does anyone have a whistle?" asked Crunch.

Most of the Chips shook their heads, but Edge knew what to do. "Mouth Guard," he began, "do you think you could . . . "

Grinning from ear to ear, Mouth Guard crouched down so his armpit was level with the mail slot. As Bond pushed the flap open, he slipped his hand through the neck of his shirt, ready to let one rip . . . just as the mayor, holding a cellphone up to her ear, opened the front door.

PPPPFFFFWWWWHHHHHHEEEEEEEEEE-EEEEET! PPPPPTHWETTTTTT!

"What was *that*?" sputtered the mayor, taken by surprise—not only by Mouth Guard's huge fart, but also by the fact that there were so many Ice Chips on her doorstep with tears in their eyes! She could barely tell who was laughing and who was crying. Behind her, Quiet Dave the Iceman, Coach Small, and Bond's dad were laughing so hard they were clutching their sides.

"Hello? I can't hear you—*hello*?" the mayor said into her phone with a shrug, trying to keep in her own giggles. But the call was already gone.

"I didn't think you'd be able to hear the doorbell with all that noise," a voice boomed from the driveway.

Lucas whipped his head around to see Mr. Blitz slipping his phone back into his pocket and striding confidently toward the mayor's front steps. The Stars' coach had Jared and Beatrice on either side of him . . . and *Lars* was shuffling behind!

"What's *he* doing here? This dinner is only for Ice Chips," Edge whispered to Lucas.

At that moment, Bond burst through the door of the mayor's house and launched herself into her father's arms.

"I don't quit! I *don't* quit!" Bond was yelling at both her dad and Coach Small, crying and wiping her eyes.

As usual, Coach Small just stood back calmly and listened.

"I didn't . . . I haven't had a chance to tell him yet," Bond's dad stammered at first. But then he started grinning when he realized what his daughter was telling him. He knew what quitting a sport felt like—what it meant—and although he'd respected Bond's decision, he really hadn't wanted her to quit the team either.

"I know I can learn to shoot now," said Bond, smiling. "I want to play! I want to be an Ice—"

"Good evening, all of you," said Mr. Blitz, interrupting. He now had one foot on the mayor's front steps and was determined to break up the scene. "Is Ingrid here?"

Lars's mom emerged from the kitchen carrying a plate of cheeses. She looked almost as surprised as Mayor Ward when she saw Mr. Blitz and the twins standing there.

"Is there something . . . wrong?" she asked, her eyes narrowing.

"Nothing, nothing. Not here to cause trouble," Mr. Blitz said with a smile as he pulled Lars out from behind him and pushed him up onto the stoop. "I've just got a few details to iron out for tomorrow's game—fireworks, catering. You know, that kind of stuff. Lars was happy when my driver picked these three up from school, but when I said we'd have to go to the rink to fix a few things, he said he'd rather go back to his mom. Apparently, Ice Chips and Stars don't hang out at rinks together—even when they *are* cousins."

At the word "cousins," Lars turned beet red.

He's related to Beatrice and Jared? Lucas actually felt sorry for the guy.

"Oh, and I guess I wanted to wish you all luck tomorrow," Mr. Blitz said as he and the twins turned to walk back toward their car, leaving Lars behind. "You'll need it."

Still standing on the steps, Lars looked at Lucas and Lucas looked at Lars, but neither of them knew what to say.

CHAPTER 18

The Chips couldn't believe the scene in front of them. Cars everywhere. The parking lot of the new arena was completely full—as though the whole town had come out. At the entrance to the Blitz Sports Complex was a massive banner: "Grand Opening!" There were lights playing off the new building, and a stage had been set up. A rock band was blaring so loudly that people walking by were forced to hold their hands over their ears.

This is bananas, Lucas thought. Mr. Blitz had gone too far. Near the front doors, he even had food trucks, a bouncy castle, and a clown walking around on gigantic stilts!

For a novice hockey game? This is way too wild, but it's also kind of . . . awesome?! Lucas felt it, but he didn't want to admit it.

"Stupendus-exaggeritis!" Edge called out as he

grabbed his hockey bag from the back of his mom's truck.

"They think they're so smart with their fancy new gear," Swift grumbled. "I want to beat them soooooooo bad."

"Do you think we'll be playing on the regular rink or the *plastic* one?" asked Lucas, already feeling depressed. Mr. Blitz's new arena was not only amazingly high-tech but also contained two full-sized, state-of-the-art rinks!

"Dunno which one . . . let's check 'em both out!" Crunch said as he took off toward the doors.

❖ ❖ ❖

"Oh—wow!" said Swift.

"They're going to *kiiiiiiill* us," said Edge, gasping.

Lucas wondered if Edge's chin would bounce off the floor. Or if Bond's eyeballs would fall out of her head. They were all standing in the new arena, staring in wonder. They'd never imagined being at such an amazing place for a novice-level hockey game.

"Which rink is ours? Which end will we start in? Does anyone have any gum?" Mouth Guard asked. He was anxious, so everything was just spilling out of his head. He'd already talked about each item in his hockey bag, told some confusing story about what he'd watched on TV last night, and wondered at length if he'd forgotten to feed his hamster, Potato, before leaving the house.

He was all over the place, but everyone else knew exactly where they were headed: to the rink where their parents were slowly taking their seats—the one with the giant puckhead mascot already dancing up and down the steps, with popcorn and cotton candy for sale, and with an amazing temperature-controlled ice surface already shining in the overhead lights.

The hallway Lucas and his friends were standing in, with their noses pressed against the windows, was really more like a glass-walled bridge. On the right, they looked down onto Mr. Blitz's synthetic rink, where several young figure skaters were being led around in a chain, all of them holding hands.

And on the left . . . they looked down at their destiny.

The Riverton Stars' new rink had a huge scoreboard with a massive full-colour, high-definition screen for replays and advertisements, and there seemed to be more seats in the stands than there were people in the whole town.

Wow . . . that ice. Lucas couldn't get over it. It wasn't magical like Scratch's ice surface—it couldn't be—but it was definitely special. It shone.

"We're in dressing room three!" Slapper called from the top of the stairs in his big, booming voice.

Lars, Dynamo, and the Face—Matias Rodriguez, the Ice Chips' second goalie—made their way past and started down the stairs toward the Ice Chips' dressing room.

"Our old rink is still better," Lucas said stubbornly, moving toward the stairs.

"Yeah, of course," agreed Crunch, but Lucas didn't believe him.

* * *

Their dressing room was huge—easily two or three times the size of the one back at the community arena. This one even had showers, just like in the pros.

"Hey, remember when Sid said that life was like one big hockey schedule? That it's either a game day or it's not a game day?" Edge asked, looking around.

"Oh, yeah. Forget the Stars' fancy jackets, I want *that* printed on a T-shirt!" Swift joked as she slid down the bench and flicked a sock at Lucas's head.

"Yeah . . . this is *definitely* a game day," Lucas said as he unzipped his hockey bag.

Once he had pulled out his skates, he kept them close—and kept his eyes on Lars. Without Mr. Johansen, the skate sharpener, around, he couldn't risk another sabotage. For this rematch, Lucas wasn't going to let Lars—or any of his equipment—out of his sight.

Lars says he's an Ice Chip, but how can he be one when the horrible Blitz twins are his cousins?!

As everyone was tightening their skates and pulling on their Ice Chips jerseys, Coach Small came in carrying a clipboard.

"Listen up," he said in his normal voice, and the Chips went quiet instantly. They had that much respect for their coach.

"Now, I know we have a lot to work on, and these exhibition games are happening earlier than we'd expected, but this new rink is a big deal for Riverton. Just try your best and I'll be more than happy. *Now let's get out there!*"

As the Ice Chips filed out the door one by one, they were so excited they were bouncing on their skates. Lucas hoped he looked that way, too—like he believed in his team and felt they had a chance of winning. Just

in case, he decided to hang back a bit, as he often did and as Sidney Crosby always did—one of their shared superstitions.

If I'm last on the ice, maybe that will make a difference?

But when Lucas moved for his turn through the door, he realized he wasn't alone in the dressing room.

"Can I talk to you?" The voice sounded shy, unsure.

And it belonged to Lars.

CHAPTER 19

Lucas and Lars were almost knocked off their skates by a blast of light and noise as they moved along after the other players, through the gate, and out onto the ice. Music was thundering down from huge speakers, the sound so loud that Lucas felt as if the drums and bass guitar were being played inside his chest.

Coach Small made his way to the visitors' bench as the Ice Chips lined up along their blue line, with Swift moving into the net.

But they were the only team on the ice.

Suddenly, the music stopped. The arena went dark. Someone in the crowd made a wolf call; a little kid started to cry.

Then the world's biggest voice filled the rink: "Ladies and gentlemen, welcome to the *amazing* Blitz Sports Complex, the state-of-the-art arena that will soon be Riverton's number-one attraction. Welcome . . . to the home of your *Stars*!"

BOOM!!!

A spotlight flashed on, blinding the Ice Chips where they stood nervously along the far blue line.

BOOM!

The music pounded down from the speakers and then faded as the huge voice came back on to introduce the Stars, now skating out one by one,

"Stars' forward, number 13, Beatrice Blitz . . . "

"At centre, number 9, Jared Blitz . . . "

The audience applauded for the players as if they were NHL greats. And then when the Stars were finally all on their blue line, the rink exploded with indoor fireworks! There was flashing and booming until the whole arena filled up with pink, white, and yellow smoke.

* * *

Soon, Lucas was skating to centre ice.

And coming toward him was Beatrice Blitz.

The Ice Chips hadn't chosen a captain yet for this year, but Coach Small had waved his hand at Lucas, telling him to take the first faceoff. Lucas didn't feel like a captain, but he kept reminding himself that back in Halifax, Sidney Crosby had told him he was good — and that must say something about his game. At least, he hoped it did.

With a huge C on her chest, Beatrice approached the circle with a laugh, dismissing Lucas before the puck had even dropped!

"I guess I don't have to touch your skates this game," she hissed, "now that we all know how bad you Chips stink."

Lucas scowled. Lars *had* been telling the truth! When he'd pulled Lucas aside on his way out of the dressing room, Lars had sworn he wasn't the one who'd sabotaged his teammate's blades. He'd said it was one of the Stars.

"If we end up on the same line today," Lars had said shyly, giving Lucas an unexpected smile, "I don't want you coming after me — I mean, we *are* on the same team."

Beatrice, however, was definitely coming after Lucas again. Her twin, Jared, probably was, too.

"Loser," Beatrice sneered as the ref leaned in between them, ready to drop the puck.

Lucas tried to breathe—to block her out.

Luckily, he had a trick, and he used it. He watched the referee's hand, not the faceoff circle, and the moment the hand released the puck, Lucas swept with his stick, catching the puck in mid-air and sending it back to Bond.

Beatrice elbowed Lucas in the helmet as she pushed past, chasing the puck. Lucas fell, scrambled back onto his skates, and waited for a whistle—but there was none. Beatrice had made it look like an accident, so the referee, who had to have seen the play, let it go.

The Chips moved the puck up, and Edge got off a shot that struck the Stars' post and rebounded back to Mouth Guard.

"Shoot!" Lucas yelled, but Mouth Guard was already moving to pass it on.

As Edge skated around behind the net, Mouth Guard drew his stick back and shot the puck over to him. But he didn't shoot it to Edge—he shot it to where Edge *had been*. Jared Blitz picked up the puck in full flight, slipped past Edge, and spun quickly around Lucas as he burst up the ice. Beatrice was skating hard, but Jared never even looked to pass. He tore over centre and swept so fast around Bond that she fell trying to turn and stay with him.

Jared then moved in on Swift, who stacked her pads to make the stop . . . but he didn't shoot! Instead, he just waited, with Swift down and out and sliding helplessly to the side. Almost as if joking, he slid the puck as slowly as a curling stone into the net—copying the only goal Lucas had made in their horrible exhibition game.

Jared then turned to skate back to the Stars' bench, laughing.

"What was that?" Edge asked Lucas as they sat on their own bench.

"I don't know," Lucas said. "But I think he's making fun of me."

Next, it was Lars's line.

Dynamo took the faceoff. He sent the puck back to Blades, who leaped at it with the grace of a figure skater and fired it over to Lars.

Moving the puck smoothly back and forth, Lars crossed centre and found himself smack in between the Blitz twins—and both were now coming for him. Blades and Dynamo moved as fast as they could down either side and were soon banging their sticks on the ice, but the moment Lars pulled back his stick, he found himself in the middle of a Blitz-twin sandwich.

The three cousins tumbled over onto the ice, and Lars cried out as the wind was knocked out of him.

"Last night you said you were an Ice Chip," Beatrice nearly spat at her cousin as she got back onto her skates. "At least now you look like one." Then she yelled out for everyone else to hear: "Sorry! Accident!"

Again, the ref let it go.

Lucas couldn't believe it.

Everything that could go wrong did go wrong for the Ice Chips. Swift had trouble controlling her rebounds, Mouth Guard's passes kept missing their marks, and Bond was unable to stop the end-to-end rushes of the Stars' big new forward—it was almost as though she was afraid of the puck. The Blitz twins both scored in the first period, and the big guy scored, too, making it 3–0 for the Stars.

At the bench, Mr. Blitz grinned and gave his new assistant coach a fist bump.

The Ice Chips were being humiliated. It looked as if it was going to be another blowout.

CHAPTER 20

When Lucas and his friends came back to the dressing room for the fresh flood that would split the game into two periods rather than their regular three—Coach Blitz wanted the flood for the TV cameras—Lars was already there, smacking his stick so hard against the wall that it broke in half. He looked like he was almost in tears.

"They did that on purpose! Jared and Bea . . . they didn't even want the puck! They just wanted me to look like a *loser*!"

"Cut it out," Swift said. "They're cheaters—get used to it."

"I won't!" Lars shouted. He'd never been on this end of Beatrice's cheating, and he'd never realized how horrible it felt—how unfair. But the other Ice Chips knew, that much was obvious. Still red in the face, Lars took a deep breath, wiped his cheeks, and went to get his second stick from the pile.

Coach Small came in behind the players, noted the broken stick lying on the floor, looked over in Lars's direction, and lifted an eyebrow that said far more than any words would have. Then he took a deep breath, too.

"The Stars might not play the way we do," Coach Small said, "but this is the team we're playing out there today—think about that. We have to play to their weaknesses. And we need to tighten up our defence."

"I *tried* to stop Jared," said Bond, starting to cry. "But I was afraid he'd take the puck from me—I almost didn't even want it!"

"If you're afraid, that is *exactly* what he'll do," said Edge. "But, Bond, you can crouch lower, protect the puck . . . don't forget the sandbag."

"The what?" asked Slapper, who was fixing the tape on his stick.

"I said don't forget the *handshake*. They've got a secret handshake now. It's for luck," Crunch said, trying to sound casual. He was a smooth talker when it came to parents, but when he talked to kids his own age, he was the worst liar ever.

Lucas shook his head—this was going nowhere.

Swift, who'd taken off her skates, got up and left the room.

"All you've got to do is try your best," said Coach Small. He had an interview to do with a TV crew out in the hallway, but he'd been trying to avoid it. Now they were banging on the door. "This next half will be better. I'll come and get you when the flood is done."

"Sid . . . er, a *guy* showed me a trick," said Mouth Guard, trying not to use Sidney Crosby's name. "He said that if I want to pass to somebody, I should look at some other player. Fake the other team out. I haven't been doing that, but I should."

"We did some of those in practice last year," said Lucas.

"Sure, but you need to be able to actually *pass* the puck for it to work," said Bond. She was being hard on herself, and she couldn't stop herself from being hard on Mouth Guard, too.

"We've only got ten minutes left in the break," said Swift, bursting back though the door with her arms full. "We'd better get moving."

Lucas's mouth dropped open—he was instantly

blown away. Swift had run upstairs and borrowed some juggling pins from the clown outside! And although she hadn't found a sandbag, Lars's broken stick had given her an idea: limbo!

When Coach Small came back to tell the kids that the flood was finished, it looked like a circus had taken over their dressing room. Mouth Guard was juggling the three coloured pins, and Bond, the Face, and Crunch were all duck-walking their way under Lars's broken stick. Swift and Edge were each holding on to an end of it, chanting, "How low can you go?"

"Guys, come on!" said Coach Small. "Focus on the game." Of course, he had no idea that was *exactly* what they were doing. "Let's go, Chips—the ice is ready!"

"So are we!" said Bond, her cheeks now flushed with excitement.

* * *

"Keep low in the corners," Lucas said, banging his stick against the back of Bond's skate as the Chips filed back onto the ice and started to take their positions. He was trying to encourage her. Even if he was the

Chips' captain only for the day, he thought he should take the role seriously.

"Are your hockey gods with us?" Bond asked, giving Lucas a wink.

"I hope so," he replied, feeling lighter. He hadn't even bitten his nails during their break.

"Then let's win this!" Edge said, grinning.

* * *

Lucas won the first faceoff and slipped out of the way of Beatrice Blitz's shoulder as she tried to plow through him. Bond got the puck over to Edge, who then slipped it to Lucas, who turned up-ice and raced over the Stars' blue line.

Lucas sussed out the situation: he could split the defence or get the puck back to Edge.

He should never have given himself a choice! In the split second between deciding and acting, the puck mysteriously vanished from Lucas's stick. It was as if a frog's long tongue had darted out and snapped a big black bug off his blade.

He turned, puzzled, only to see Beatrice scooting back toward the Chips' end. She was in full flight and had just dropped the puck from her blade back into her skates when Bond, out of nowhere, reached out and scooped it away.

As fast as she could, Bond moved into the corner and crouched down over the puck, just as Sid had told her to do. She was shorter than Beatrice, but now she'd use that to her advantage. Bond moved left, then right, keeping her back to the Stars' captain, and then fired the puck down the ice with a solid flick of her wrist.

The round black disc was flying a good foot above the ice surface when Mouth Guard plucked it out of the air.

Jared was immediately on Lucas, and the other Stars had the Ice Chips covered. The only one open was Bond, who was charging up the ice, looking as determined as she had pulling that sandbag in the Citadel.

Her head was low and she was moving—as fast as a train.

Mouth Guard made like he was passing to Lucas and instead fired toward the far side of the net. The puck was sliding up toward the crease—and Bond was there to meet it! A perfect pass!

With Beatrice chasing after her, Bond swept in on the goalie and pulled him out. She leaned on her back foot, rolled her wrist like Sid had taught her, and quickly roofed a shot off the crossbar.

Now it was 3–1, with the Stars still ahead.

Dynamo got lucky and scored next. Then Edge slammed one top shelf.

Now they were tied—three for the Chips, and three for the Stars.

Coach Small started to juggle his lines, hoping to find a combination that might help them even more.

"Lars," he said, tapping him on the shoulder, "you're on with Edge and Lucas."

Lucas almost choked. The coach wasn't looking to put Lars into Lucas's position this time—he wanted them to be *linemates*!

Right away, the puck was shot down into the Chips' end. Bond seized it and skated behind Swift's net, waiting for Lucas to swoop in and grab it.

As Lucas rounded the net with the puck, he looked up-ice to see Beatrice Blitz coming over the boards from the Stars' bench!

He quickly passed to his best friend on the backhand. Edge snatched the puck and made a move as if he were going to stickhandle over the blue line, but instead he just left the puck sitting there while he straddled the line, careful not to go offside. Lucas recognized it: this was their drop-pass play.

Moving fast, Lucas picked up the puck again and saw that Beatrice was rushing straight at him. He moved to the left, toward the boards, and did something he knew better than to do—he fired a nearly blind backhand pass across the ice. He was sure he had seen something. No, not quite sure. More like . . . hopeful.

But Lars had read him perfectly! He'd sensed what Lucas was going to do and darted for that open ice on the other side. The puck came through from Lucas, and Lars picked it up in full stride on the absolute centre of his blade. He moved in on the net, faked forehand to backhand, and ripped a goal in off the Stars' post.

It was 4–3 for the Ice Chips!

The arena erupted in cheers. The Ice Chips were ahead!

Lucas couldn't believe it. All the Chips were rushing at Lars, who was in the corner with his back to the boards and his arms in the air.

Lucas skated over to them. His eyes briefly met Lars's, and without even thinking, Lucas jumped at him, throwing an arm around his neck.

"YESSSSS!!!"

❖ ❖ ❖

"See you tonight!" Bond said to Lars as she swung her bag up onto her shoulder and slipped through the door of the dressing room. Her dad had told her she could have some of her teammates over to celebrate their win. And this time, they'd have two nets: Swift in one and the Shooter Tutor in the other.

"You going?" Lars asked, looking up at Lucas, who was just putting on his coat. Lars had never used a Shooter Tutor before, but he was glad Bond had invited him. "You know, I heard that Sidney Crosby shot into a dryer in his parents' basement to practise."

Lucas paused, holding on to his zipper. "Actually, Sid didn't shoot *into* the dryer—he just hit it by accident because it was behind his net." As he spoke, he realized that meant Sidney Crosby—the *great* Sidney Crosby—hadn't made all of his shots either.

"Hey, Lucas?" said Swift, once Lars had left to join his mother. The only kids now in the dressing room with her were Lucas, Edge, and Mouth Guard. "The real season starts next week—we'll have our first game. We met Sid, and that's awesome. But I was thinking . . ."

"You want to leap again," Lucas blurted. He'd seen it coming from a mile away.

"I'm in!" cried Mouth Guard.

"Me, *toodle-oo!*" cheered Edge.

"Good," said Swift, grinning at all her friends. "But that armpit's not coming with us, okay?" she added, her eyes resting on Mouth Guard. "And since you all got to meet Sid, *your* idol," she continued, smiling. "Next time, it's *my* turn."

ACKNOWLEDGEMENTS

Thank you to Suzanne Sutherland for helping us grab hold of this hurricane and shape it, for her thoughtful edits, and for shepherding us through our first *Ice Chips* book signing. Thanks to Maeve O'Regan in publicity for her amazing ideas and enthusiasm; to Kaitlyn Vincent and Ashley Posluns in marketing; and to Editorial Director Jennifer Lambert for her support. And thanks to the rest of the amazing team at HarperCollins, who allowed us to leap through time once again: Janice Weaver, our careful copyeditor; Stephanie Nuñez, our helpful and well-organized production editor; and Lloyd Davis, our keen-eyed proofreader. Thank you also to Bruce Westwood and Meg Wheeler at Westwood Creative Artists for their guidance and friendship.

Thanks to the many friends and new acquaintances who lent us their stories so we could shape the story of Tianna "Bond" Foster: Stephanie MacGregor, the aunt who makes the best curried anything; Camille and Roger Dundas, friends and co-founders of ByBlacks.com; Toronto playwright Teneile Warren; and Kerry's American in Paris, Kymberli Stewart.

Thank you also to Kim Smith, whose beautiful and inspired art wows us every time.

And thank you to our families, who let us create mini-hurricanes around the house whenever we were stuck in writing mode.

And finally — not wanting to give anything away — thank you to young Sid for providing the world of hockey with such a lovely anecdote.

—Roy MacGregor and Kerry MacGregor

Many thanks to Roy MacGregor and Kerry MacGregor for creating another magical story; to Suzanne Sutherland, who brought everything together; to Kelly Sonnack, my amazing agent; and to my husband, Eric, for answering even more questions about hockey.

—Kim Smith

ROY MACGREGOR, who was the media inductee into the Hockey Hall of Fame in 2012, has been described by the *Washington Post* as "the closest thing there is to a poet laureate of Canadian hockey." He is the author of the internationally successful Screech Owls hockey mystery series for young readers, which has sold more than two million copies and is also published in French, Chinese, Swedish, Finnish, and Czech. It is the most successful hockey series in history—and is second only to *Anne of Green Gables* as a Canadian book series for young readers—and, for two seasons, was a live-action hit on YTV. MacGregor has twice won the ACTRA Award for best television screenwriting.

KERRY MACGREGOR is co-author of the latest work in the Screech Owls series. She has worked in news and current affairs at the CBC, and as a journalist with the *Toronto Star*, the *Ottawa Citizen*, and many other publications. Her columns on parenting, written with a unique, modern perspective on the issues and interests of today's parents, have appeared in such publications as *Parenting Times* magazine.

KIM SMITH is an illustrator from Calgary. She is the *New York Times*–bestselling illustrator of over thirty picture books, including *Boxitects*, the Builder Brother series, and the Pop-Classics picture book adaptations of popular films, including *Back to the Future*, *Home Alone*, and *E.T. the Extra-Terrestrial*. Growing up, Kim's favourite hockey player was Lanny McDonald. She still admires his iconic moustache to this day.

MORE ICE CHIPS MAGIC!

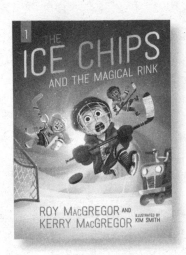

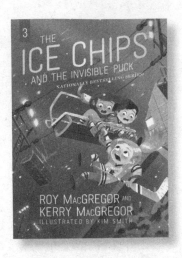